FINAL VICTORY

THE SHACKLEFORD DIARIES

BOOK SEVEN

BEVERLEY WATTS

Cover design by Dar Albert at wickedsmartdesigns.com

CHAPTER 1

I should have known it would come to light eventually. This kind of juicy gossip is gold dust to the tabloids. Of course, I didn't realise the headlines would be quite so lurid, but then perhaps I'm just lacking in imagination.

And the timing couldn't have been worse. The story broke this morning, on the very day I'm to be Best Woman at my only friend's wedding. Truthfully, Alex is likely to be my *ex*-only friend if the paparazzi end up chasing the wedding party, waiting for a glimpse of the fourteenth Duke of Blackmore together with his sumo wrestling girlfriend. And no, I'm not, nor ever have been, a sumo wrestler – but this morning's papers have had a high old time with the whole *like mother like daughter* thing. And as my uncle Charlie is so fond of saying – Never let the truth get in the way of a good story.

In case you're wondering how a sumo-wrestler's daughter managed to bag a drop dead gorgeous, silver-haired, whisky eyed peer of the realm whose path is customarily littered with the prone bodies of women swooning at the sight of him (well, every Friday during *Dinner with the Duke* anyway), I'd have to answer that I've no bloody idea.

I mean, to be fair, I've never expected our relationship to last forever, but once he knows the *whole* sordid story, he might decide to cut and run sooner rather than later...

But right now, I have a twenty-four-hour reprieve because Alex and Freddy's wedding is taking place on the edge of a cliff at the end of a two-mile track that absolutely no car bigger than a mini is going to be able to access easily. Not to mention the labyrinth of narrow Devon roads that any intrepid reporter would have to navigate to even reach said narrow two-mile track.

And since the majority of the wedding party is already in situ, my fingers and toes are firmly crossed that the media circus will be mostly delayed until the day after the wedding.

* * *

'BLOODY HELL, Jimmy, it's at times like this I have to seriously question your ancestry. I thought you said your great granddad was a navigator. If that's not complete bollocks, you certainly haven't been blessed with his genes.'

'The satnav's not working, Sir. The hedges are too high.'

'I'm going to send for one of those DNA thingies – you know, where you suck on a stick, and they can tell you who your ancestors are,' Emily confided to Mabel in the back of the car. 'I thought it would be a nice early Christmas present for Jimmy.'

'Does the kit tell you if they were human or not?' muttered the Admiral from the front as Jimmy squinted at his phone while giving his armpit a quick scratch.

'Ooh, how interesting,' enthused Mabel. 'Perhaps I should get Charlie one. I mean, now it looks as though he could be related to a real Duke.'

'They're buy one, get one free at the moment, so we can get one each,' Emily suggested.

'I think we have to turn left here,' Jimmy mumbled, 'and the lane to the hotel should be about a mile down this road.'

'Let's hope so, Jimmy lad. I'm too bloody old to be driving into ditches.'

'Are you having a didgeridoo moment, Charlie?' Mabel piped up from the back. 'So am I. This really does look just the same as the road leading up to that lighthouse we stayed in up in north Devon. Do you remember, Emily?'

The Admiral sighed and gave his fiancée an irritated look through the mirror. 'Well, I just hope we don't need towing out of this bollocking mess. I don't know what possessed Freddy to get hitched somewhere that's more difficult to get to than the bloody moon.'

'Well, at least the reporters aren't likely to find it either,' Emily commented.

The Admiral frowned as he turned the car towards the left. 'What reporters? Have they got wind that the Yank'll be there?'

Jimmy turned to his former superior officer in surprise. 'Haven't you read the papers this morning, Sir?'

'I've hardly had the time,' the Admiral responded testily. 'What with getting ready for this bloody wedding and picking you and Emily up.' He glanced over at Jimmy expectantly. When the small man didn't speak, he added, 'Well, spit it out Jimmy, we haven't got all bollocking day. I'm ready for a pint and Pickles's legs are likely in plaits.' The Springer spaniel gave an enthusiastic whine from his customary place in between Mabel and Emily.

'Well, the thing is, Sir, I think the tabloids have discovered Teddy's mother's ... err... unusual profession – and you know, with her courting the Duke and all...' He trailed off.

The Admiral raised his eyebrows and gave a rude snort. 'I should think they're having a bloody field day with that.'

'Well, yes – the headlines have been actually quite inventive,' Jimmy responded with a reluctant chuckle.

'If they're that bad, his grace might well be giving Teddy her marching orders. I hope she won't be looking to move back in with me and Mabel.' The car screeched to a sudden halt as he caught sight of a sign on a large gate.

'Does that say Sugar Rock Hotel?' he mumbled, peering at the sign and fumbling for his glasses. Jimmy wound down the window and stuck his head out. 'I think this is the place, Sir,' he responded, climbing out of the car to open the gate. The Admiral watched the small man scrambling around in satisfaction. It was good to see order restored once in a while.

Seconds later, they were easing through the opening, and after shutting the gate behind them, Jimmy climbed back into the car.

Keeping his eyes firmly on the narrow track and watching out for any big boulders, the Admiral turned the conversation back to the tabloids' latest revelations.

'I wonder what happened to Agnes. I reckon Teddy hasn't seen her for donkey's years.'

'Well, that's the thing, Sir. It looks as though a reporter's located Teddy's mother. According to the article I read this morning, The *Mail's* got an exclusive. It's going to be in tomorrow's edition.'

* * *

'WHAT DO YOU MEAN, she's done an interview?' My voice goes up an octave, disturbing the lone seagull who's been eying the Danish pastry I've just picked up from the buffet table.

'That's all I know, Teddy love. And the only reason I'm even aware of it is because the newspaper wanted to hear my side of the story.'

Why the bloody hell did I think it was a good idea to call my dad?

'I assume you told them where to put their damn story.' My curt tone is not a question as I fight to push down the anger and hurt that's lain dormant in my body since my mother's disappearance.

'I've got no intention of talking to any newspapers,' my father responds indignantly. 'I can't imagine what your mother thinks she's doing, opening up that can of bloody worms.'

'Well, she's hardly likely to give them the truth, Dad. But at the end of the day, she's a greedy bitch, and I've no doubt she'll come up with a story that will sell newspapers.' I bite my lip to stifle the urge to scream. This is so much worse than my original assessment. I hope Sebastian manages to make it here without having to run the damn gauntlet.

'Once the wedding gets underway, I won't be able to answer the phone,' I inform my father. 'Whatever you do, say nothing. We know how this works, we've had nearly thirty years practice. If you need to, leave me an answerphone message and I'll get back to you as soon as I can.'

I can almost feel him nodding. 'What are you going to tell that Duke of yours?'

I sigh. 'I've spent the whole of my adult life pretending the whole thing never happened. But that dubious luxury's gone now. I have to tell him the truth, Dad. I owe him that at least.'

With a last grimace, I cut the call and make my way outside to the rest of the wedding party.

'I was under the impression it was your mother who was the sumo wrestler.' Kit's comment is accompanied by a frown as she looks up from the morning paper.

My eyes narrow as I take in the scene in front of me. Of the ten people sitting on the hotel terrace, only four don't have a newspaper in front of them – and three of those can't actually read.

My cousin Victory looks over at me, the sympathy obvious in her eyes – she's all too familiar with the damage newspapers can do to a relationship.

Sighing, I sit down. 'I'm not, and never have been into any kind of wrestling. God, I need coffee.'

'I'll order a fresh pot.' Alex climbs to his feet with a supportive smile.

'Well, if any paparazzi manage to find their way here, they're welcome to whatever photos they can get just for ingenuity,' Freddy comments with a wink. 'You'll just have to make sure you stay at all times on my good side.' The last is obviously directed at me.

'I doubt very much they'll put that much effort in,' I scoff.

'Oh, you'd be surprised,' Tory pipes up, obviously speaking from experience. I can't help but smile as I watch her spoon feeding the twins. At eleven months, they are like peas in a pod. Girls, as Tory predicted long before they were born. I think back to their birth. They were nearly a month early - as many twins are - and were actually born on different days. The oldest popped out in the last few minutes of October – hence her name of October (Tobi for short - she'll be so grateful when she gets older). Twin number two wasn't born for another hour and a half - obviously having decided that she was warm and comfortable exactly where she was, thank you very much. And yes, they called her November which apparently is very popular in the States. I have to say I much prefer the shortened version of Ember. She'll be even more grateful than her sister by the time she learns to talk...

Naturally, the Admiral's comments were unrepeatable.

'It'll blow over as soon as the next big story comes along,' Noah predicts, handing Isaac another piece of toast, avidly watched by their little dog Dotty, who might be getting on in years, but certainly hasn't lost her flair for putting herself in pole position for snack retrieval.

Obviously, being a world-famous actor, Noah's our resident authority on the vagaries of the paparazzi. He doesn't know about my mother's interview yet – none of them do, and I have no intention of saying anything until the wedding is done and dusted.

I give another sigh. 'I'm so sorry this has surfaced on the day of your wedding, guys. You can throw me out if you like. Replace me as Best Woman.'

Freddy raises his eyebrow. 'Darling,' he drawls, 'aside from the fact that I'm marrying the man of my dreams, this has to be the most exciting thing to happen since Tory bagged the world's sexiest actor. We could be on tomorrow's front page.'

'You mean to tell me you weren't excited when Kit bagged herself a braw highlander?' Jason interrupts with mock affront. 'I'm truly gutted. But then of course, you're all Sassenachs.'

'Well, as much as my appreciation knows no bounds at such a miraculous honour, this Sassenach needs to pee,' Kit announces, holding her hand out for Jason to heave her out of her chair. 'Why didn't you tell me about the incessant bladder issues that come with pregnancy?' she grumbles to Tory.

Freddy frowns, a sudden thought obviously piercing his dreams of superstardom 'In all honesty, if I had ready replacements, I'd be binning you and Tory,' he declares with a sniff. 'One bridesmaid walking down the aisle with an appendage on each hip, the second sporting a bump bigger than Texas.' He gives a dramatic sigh and holds out his hand for another Bucks Fizz. 'I dread to think what the newspaper photos will look like.'

'Truly your altruism is breathtaking,' Kit retorts. 'Of course, the key to that whole speech is *if you had ready replacements*. Which you don't. So, suck it up buttercup. You're stuck with us.' She gives him an evil grin as she makes her ponderous way towards the ladies.

'And hormonal to boot,' Freddy yells after her.

'Well, you could always ask Mabel and Emily,' Tory adds, not at all offended, 'I'm certain they're on their way as we speak.'

Freddy favours her with a deadpan stare as he takes a sip of his Bucks Fizz. 'You are tolerated for your connections, not your rapier wit,' he comments loftily.

Tory laughs out loud and leans forward to press a kiss against his cheek. 'Never change, Freddy,' she murmurs.

The affection in her voice is obvious, and for a moment, I actually think Freddy's going to cry, until seconds later he looks down at himself and wails, 'Oh my God, I can't believe you've just got rusk all over my Paul Smith shirt. That's it, connections or no, our friendship is over...'

His lamenting is cut short as the waitress comes with a fresh pot of coffee. She favours Noah with a coquettish smile as she hands me a cup, very nearly spilling the whole lot in my lap. I instinctively watch to see Tory's reaction to such blatant flirting, thinking if the woman was gazing at Sebastian like she wanted to eat him, I'd be tempted to lamp her one. Tory simply smiles at her sweetly, asks for her name and tells her what a wonderful job she's doing.

I fight the urge to grin at the waitress's confusion. Clearly, I have a lot to learn...!

Abruptly, I realise that I haven't actually thought about my mother at all in the last ten minutes and feel the customary warm fuzzy that seems to have characterised most of my interactions since coming to Dartmouth.

It's hard to believe I've actually been here for over a year - aside from two weeks Seb and I spent in the South of France with Tory and Noah while he was filming his latest movie.

The time has passed unbelievably quickly. After the furore created by Sebastian's ex-wife, Carla, last summer, our relationship has ... let's say it's been progressing - slowly. I think we're both wary of any kind of firm commitment. Seb after being married to a money grabbing nutcase, and me …? Well, I think anybody who gets within striking distance becomes very quickly aware I have major trust issues. Prickly doesn't even begin to cover it. And when you add in the fact that Sebastian is so far above my pay grade, it's almost laughable, *and* that this relationship is really the only one I've ever had …

Which is why my contentment in my little shed (sorry – chalet) in my employer's garden is bizarre, to say the least. But there we are.

Since looking into the Sinclair family history when I first started my job as chief reporter for the Dartmouth Herald - yep that really is my title - every single job at the Herald has been relatively mundane. I say *relatively*. Alex and I did actually unearth the whereabouts of old Harold Parkinson's mother. It turns out she's alive and well, living in Croydon.

And you know what? I don't actually care. The old Teddy who needed the constant adrenaline rush to prove she was alive is well and truly buried. I might still be prickly, but my suicidal urges to rush headlong into danger have finally gone. I'm happy – or I was, until the juicy gossip about my mother surfaced.

Unwilling to lose myself down that particular rabbit hole again, I drag my thoughts back to the present. Alex and Freddy are tying the knot in a delightfully out-of-the-way boutique hotel with glorious views over the sea and the entrance to the River Dart. They've kept the guest list small, inviting close family and friends only – which is probably a good thing since it keeps the number of guests wandering around the narrow Devon lanes until they end up driving off a cliff to a minimum.

Both men are only children. Freddy's parents popped their clogs a while ago, so his family bit consists of an eighty-five-year-old aunt from Kingsbridge (to be honest, the chances of her actually finding the hotel are remote at best). Both Alex's parents are here as well as his Uncle Delroy from Jamaica, but that's the grand total of his relatives. Fortunately, however, both men have enough friends in Dartmouth to completely fill all the other rooms in the hotel.

It's a beautiful morning in late September. The leaves on the shrubbery surrounding the secluded patio are just beginning to turn golden, and beyond, we can just about hear the faint sound of the sea crashing onto the cliffs below. In the distance are Dartmouth and Kingswear Castles, hazy sentinels at the entrance to the River Dart. The whole thing is truly magical – or would be if Freddy wasn't still wailing about his Paul Smith shirt.

'Were you intending to get married in that particular shirt?' I ask, since everybody else seems to be ignoring his histrionics.

Freddy sniffs and gives me a wounded look before muttering, 'That's not the point.'

'Don't worry about it, Freddy, I'll get the stain out.' Tory waves unsympathetically towards the distraught groom.

Freddy gives a rude snort. 'As if I'd give you any of my clothes to clean. Didn't Isaac's shirt start out white?' he waves towards his godson, who's now liberally covered in jam and butter.

'It's still white,' Tory protests.

'No, honey, under the jam, it's a delightful shade of pale blue.' Noah grins at his beloved's indignant face.

'Isn't it about time you were soaking in a hot bath, getting ready for our big day?' Alex laughs.

'Your insensitivity does not bode well,' Freddy grumps at his fiancé. 'And anyway, I shouldn't even be seeing you before the ceremony.'

'You'd better get going then,' Alex responds, bending down to kiss the top of Freddy's head. 'Don't keep me waiting,' he murmurs softly. 'This is the best day of my life.'

Freddy bites his lip, all stroppiness abruptly dissolving. 'Mine too,' he mumbles hoarsely, climbing to his feet.

'Send us a text when you're ready for us to come pretty you up,' Kit smiles.

'As if either of you know the first thing about style,' is Freddy's scornful parting shot.

CHAPTER 2

I've never been a ditherer. Throughout my whole life, I've always taken the bull by the horns and bugger the consequences.

So why on this particular occasion can I not seem to get the necessary words past my gritted teeth? It's not like Sebastian doesn't know about the newspaper revelations, and, really, it's not as if she'll likely to tell the bloody truth in tomorrow's interview.

I mean, to be honest, I could just continue to bury the whole thing back deep in its box – the one securely locked and gathering dust in the distant recesses of my mind…

But there's the other oddity about me. I absolutely hate lying. And forthright is my middle name. While the file labelled, *My Mother* remained in the furthest reaches of my head, I could simply ignore it. But now it's been dragged out into the open, I don't have that luxury anymore. And Sebastian really does deserve the whole sordid truth.

So why does the thought of telling him bring me out in a cold sweat?

The truth is, I'm terrified. Me, the original *I don't give a shit*, Theodora Shackleford is frightened to death of losing the best thing that's ever happened to me. There I've said it.

The reception is in full swing. The ceremony earlier was suitably tear-inducing and the wedding breakfast divine. I could blame my reluctance to speak up on the fact that I don't want to cause a scene. But I know that's bullshit. Seb would fall on his sword rather than make a public spectacle of himself – British aristocracy are trained from the cradle in the whole stiff upper lip thing. And despite being one of the few Dukes left with an inherited title, the limelight's never held any interest for him.

He also has a mother who's more eccentric than mine. Although, to my knowledge she's never *knowingly* broken the law.

I sigh and look down at my now empty glass. I can hear Sebastian's deep laugh all the way from the bar. He's talking to Noah and Jason before they call it a night. Both Tory and Kit have already retired to their rooms. Tory to get her three gusset gremlins to bed (and I happen to know she has a bottle of Moet and Chandon on ice in the room) and Kit because she's seven months pregnant and suffering from terrible heartburn.

Of course, when she admitted it to Freddy, he took great satisfaction in informing her that it likely meant she was going to give birth to a hairy baby. Her sour retort was that if that was the case, she was about to give birth to Chewbacca. Apparently, the only thing that helps it is to spend as much time horizontal as possible. On a positive note, she and Jason finally managed to employ an excellent hotel manager for Bloodstone Tower at the same time the morning sickness set in.

So now, Seb and I finally have the table to ourselves. I've got no more excuses…

'What's this about old Agnes airing her loin cloth in public?' My heart sinks as I look up at the looming figure of my Uncle Charlie. Damn. I thought I'd done so well avoiding what I had no doubt would be an uncomfortable tête-à-tête.

Which makes my next words all the more inexplicable. Especially the hysterical laugh – it takes a lot to make the Admiral visibly flinch.

'That's nothing, Uncle Charlie. You wait until the *Yakuza* connection comes to light…'

* * *

IT'S NEARLY MIDNIGHT. I'm sitting up in bed covertly watching the lamplight turn Sebastian's hair to burnished silver as he moves about the room, slowly removing his clothes. I really don't think he knows how sexy he looks, he's just been blessed with an innate grace that's as natural to him as breathing. Along with eyes that would tempt a saint.

Biting my lip, I force back the carnal thoughts clamouring for attention inside my head. As much as I'm desperate to lose myself in his touch, I need to unburden myself first. Gritting my teeth, I put my hand down to stroke Coco, allowing her soft snores to bring me back to the matter at hand.

'Seb, we need to talk.' I manage to stammer hoarsely at length.

He turns to look at me. *'Finally,'* is all he says with a sigh. 'I was beginning to think I'd have to hold you down and force you to open up.'

'I'm nearly as tall as you. How on earth would you force me?' I scoff, trying to ignore the sudden slam of pure sensation deep in my core, as well as the knowledge that he'd been well aware that I'd been holding something back from him the whole time.

He walks over to me and sits down on the edge of the bed, his incredible eyes holding mine. Then lifting his hand, he gently pushes back my hair as I gaze at him, mesmerised. For a second, he simply stares into my eyes, then, bending his head to place a soft kiss on my neck he murmurs, 'I've brought the fluffy pink handcuffs.'

For a moment his words don't quite register, then I feel his laughter and push him away indignantly. He rocks back slightly, then enfolds me in his arms. 'Tell me.'

I rest my head on his broad chest as I try to gather my thoughts. My heart is galloping like a mad thing, and in the end, it's a good two minutes before I begin. He doesn't badger me, simply waits.

'My mother ...' I start, then stop, having no idea where to go from here. In the end, I just say it. 'When we lived in Japan, my mother wasn't just a sumo wrestler, I think she worked for the *Yakuza*.'

Sebastian sits back and stares at me, frowning. Of all the things he expected me to say, that clearly didn't make the cut.

'Dad and I had no idea – until she disappeared one day. Turns out she went into hiding with her ... well, we don't really know what he was exactly – her lover, business partner, both.' I give a shrug.

Seb opens his mouth to speak, but I lay my fingers gently on his lips. He nods in understanding and allows me to continue.

'We had a *visit*. They searched the house, pretty much ransacked the place. Then we were strongly advised to leave Japan. Dad had no idea what my mother had been up to. Our lifestyle hardly reeked of laundered money. I don't think he wanted to abandon her, but in the end his fear for me won out. Two weeks later we landed in Heathrow Airport.' I stop and give another shrug. 'The last time I heard from my mother was twenty-nine years ago. She kissed me on the head as I left for school and told me to work hard.'

'Do you think your mother's in danger with the newspaper revelations?' Sebastian asks, wasting no time on inane questions. I shake my head.

'There's nothing really new in the story – I doubt the *Yakuza* would be interested. It's old news really. They're well aware she had a daughter, but they've never shown any interest in me at all. Truthfully, all these years I thought she was very likely buried in an unmarked grave somewhere.'

He makes no comment on my cold-blooded statement. 'I take it the NCA had no idea of your mother's criminal connections.' I shake my head.

'Naturally, I didn't put it on my CV.' I sigh before adding, 'Agnes wasn't much of a mother, even when she was present. I missed her when we first came to England, but not for long. And truthfully, I've not given her much thought until now.'

Sebastian is quiet for a moment, and I decide to give him time to mull over my words before I drop the bombshell.

'The story will be a five-minute wonder,' he says eventually. 'You know that. And you're not the kind of person who gives a damn what anybody thinks or says. So aside from your concern for my tender sensibilities, there's something you haven't told me yet, so spill.'

Did I mention he's also not stupid?

I take a deep breath then swallow. 'The *Mail* says they have an exclusive interview with my mother. It's apparently to be published in tomorrow's ...' I glance down at my watch, *'today's* edition.' He stares at me silently, sorting through the ramifications of what I've just said.

'I can't imagine she's going to come clean about her *Yakuza* connections,' he offers at length.

'Me neither. But what if she does? It will put a completely different light on our relationship, Seb. It won't just be mildly amusing anymore.' I grip his hands when he doesn't speak. 'I don't know what the hell she's been up to in the last thirty years. Has she been running from the *Yakuza* all this time? She must have a bloody compelling reason to break cover, and she might be a greedy bitch, but I can't imagine they're paying her that much.'

'It depends how juicy the story is,' he responds thoughtfully. 'If she's going to dish the dirt on the biggest crime organisation in Japan, they might well be giving her an open cheque.'

My carefully bolstered defences crumble under his matter-of-fact comment. Not for one second had I considered she might actually be so bloody *stupid*. I grip his hands feverishly. 'You have to leave now. Put as much distance between us as you can …' I pause, then shake my head. 'No, it's me. I have to leave. I'm putting all of you in danger just by being here, I have to …'

'Teddy, *stop*.' His command actually has me pausing mid outburst. 'We have no idea what the article is going to say.' He stops and places his hands on either side of my face, gently but firmly. 'We'll deal with this *together*.' His emphasis on the word together, warms and chills me in equal measure. 'Running off half-cocked won't solve anything. And it certainly won't protect the people who love you. We're undoubtedly already on their radar. It will wait until morning.'

'It's already morning,' I whisper, unable to contain my anguish now I'd let my deepest fear out of its box. 'How on earth will I be able to sleep between now and the morning papers?'

'I wasn't thinking of sleeping,' he murmurs leaning forward and placing the softest of kisses on my lips. His hands slip down onto my shoulders, kneading and massaging, before sliding down the front of me and settling over my breasts. His thumbs stroke my nipples through the satin and despite my fear, the response is instant. His kiss deepens and with a small whimper I respond, opening my mouth to his, seeking the kind of oblivion only Sebastian has ever given me.

I feel him slide the camisole off my shoulders and gasp against his mouth as his fingers touch my bare skin. Then he gently pushes me backwards until I'm lying across the bed. I vaguely feel Coco jump off. Clever girl knows when to head to her basket. Then Sebastian takes my right nipple into his mouth, and I stop thinking altogether…

* * *

'Why didn't you tell us your mother's a celebrity?' The disappointment in Freddy's voice is almost comical, especially as he prides himself on knowing absolutely everything.

'Did you know your mother was being interviewed by the *Sunday Fail?*' Alex's tone is much more concerned.

I simply grin at them both. Nothing can take away my euphoria on reading this morning's *Mail.* The long and the short of it? The article is full of humorous anecdotes about her time in the Japanese ring. Very little about me and Dad and nothing at all about organised crime. To say I was relieved would be putting it mildly. Clearly, she'd made peace with the *Yakuza,* or at least was no longer a person of interest to them. According to the newspaper, she's a bit of an urban legend on the Japanese sumo wrestling circuit. Apparently, she hasn't been seen for years. I can only assume she did the interview for the money. Perhaps her ill-gotten gains are dwindling.

But whatever her reason, I can now forget about her entirely and get on with my life.

The only fly in the ointment was the conversation I had with my father first thing this morning. He hadn't been quite as euphoric as me. Said he couldn't understand why she'd taken such a risk. There was nothing of substance in the piece, so she really couldn't have earned much. When I suggested that perhaps she was no longer on the *Yakuza's* hit list, he'd scoffed and said that from the little he'd learned during his time in Japan, *nobody* ever came off it.

'We hear nothing for almost thirty years, then as soon as the story breaks about your relationship with Sebastian, she comes out of the woodwork,' was his dubious comment.

'Perhaps she's planning a spot of blackmail,' I suggested sarcastically.

'Well, if she is, she's given all her bloody cards away.' I could almost see my father's disbelieving shrug.

'Dad, whatever her motives, they're nothing to do with us. She left us years ago. Please tell me you're not still carrying some kind of torch for her?'

He gave a rude snort, much to my relief. 'No, I don't give a carrot. I'm just …' he paused before giving a loud sigh and adding, 'worrying unduly, I'm sure.'

'I think you are, Dad. I admit I was anxious yesterday,' I confessed, putting my hysterical reaction of last night down to an excess of alcohol and a fertile imagination. 'But, I mean, what's the worst she can do?'

'She could write a book.' I admit my father's dry response did give me a slight sense of foreboding.

'Can we just let this go, Dad?' I pleaded. 'Without any more fuel on the fire, it will all go away, and we can just go back to normal.'

'Bloody hell, girl, who are you and what have you done with my daughter? I never thought I'd see the day you preferred *normal*. That Duke of yours has certainly done a number on you.'

'How do you know my change of heart has anything to do with Sebastian,' I responded waspishly.

'Well, it's certainly not Charlie's influence, so who else could it be …?'

'I happen to have family other than an eccentric uncle here, Dad. And … well, I have *friends* in Dartmouth too.' I have to say the word friends did stick in my throat a little – it's not a word I've used much throughout my life. A couple of minutes later we said our goodbyes, and I put the entire conversation firmly out of my mind.

'Sounds like your ma's had a colourful life,' Noah adds with a grin. 'You think she'd agree to a movie?' Then he laughs out loud at my look of horror.

'I knew about the article yesterday, but didn't want any more revelations about my mother to spoil your day. In fact, I think from now on, the less said about her, the better,' I retort. 'I would be eternally grateful if you would respond with a no comment should any of you get quizzed by an overzealous reporter.'

'Well, no reporter who values his balls is likely to come within a hundred feet of me,' Tory declares flippantly.

'Well, it's not as if you've ever had a queue of men with high opinions of their tackle beating down your door, sweetie.' Freddy pops an almond croissant into his mouth with a wink.

'Neither have you,' Tory retorts with a saccharine smile.

'Don't worry, Teddy, you have no cause to worry. Our lips are sealed.' Kit crosses her hand over her heart.

'Of course, if they want any dirt on Sebastian, well, that's a different matter,' grins Jason.

'I'm afraid all my dodgy linen has been well and truly aired.' Seb's response is dry.

The mention of airing items of clothing reminds me of my rash comments to the Admiral the night before. A sudden sense of foreboding creeps over me as I realise he's not in the dining room. In fact, neither are Mabel, Jimmy and Emily. 'Where's Uncle Charlie?' I ask, hoping he's just decided to have a lie in.

'He dragged the other three off straight after they'd finished breakfast,' Tory shrugs, accustomed to the idiosyncrasies of her father. 'Said something important had come up.'

'And you weren't concerned?' My voice comes out a little shrill, and she raises her eyebrows at my tone before staring at me thoughtfully.

'Now you come to mention it...' She frowns, bending down to pick up the spoon Tobi's just dropped, beating Dotty to it by seconds.

I realise they still know nothing about my mother's Japanese gangland connections.

Unlike the Admiral. Whose middle name is Gung-ho.

I feel sick.

CHAPTER 3

'Well, Sir, if Agnes Shackleford really does have connections to a criminal organisation, I really think we should think twice about getting involved.' Jimmy waved at the morning newspaper in his lap. 'And since there's no mention of anything remotely illegal in this interview, I doubt very much there's even a story to investigate. What did Teddy say exactly?'

The Admiral frowned. 'She just said her mother was connected to the *Yakuza*. I mean with all that racket going on, we didn't exactly have a cosy chat.'

'Ooh, a jacuzzi,' Mabel piped up from the back. 'Do you think Teddy would let us use it?'

'Have you got your hearing aids in Mabel? The *Yakuza* is Japan's largest crime organisation, not a bollocking hot tub.'

'Oh, that's a shame,' the matron sighed, not in the least offended by her fiancé's less than charitable tone. 'I think it might have done my bunion good.'

'I think Jimmy's right,' Emily interjected. 'Most likely Teddy's mother has turned over a new leaf and the Japanese criminal fraternity have forgotten all about her.'

'If you'd ever met Agnes, you'd never forget it,' the Admiral grumbled. 'She's got a face like a bag of spanners.'

'Oh, I don't think she looked that bad in the paper,' Emily protested, holding her hand out to have another look.

'That's because you can only see the back of her,' the Admiral scoffed as Jimmy obligingly held the newspaper over his shoulder. 'I doubt our Bill ever got a wink of bloody sleep the whole time they were married.'

'Well, Teddy certainly doesn't take after her,' Emily retorted.

'Teddy doesn't take after Bill either. I reckon she's more like me if I'm honest.'

'Charlie, that's a dreadful thing to say,' Mabel declared with a wink at Emily.

The Admiral just scowled at her through the rear-view mirror.

'Quite frankly, Sir, as intriguing as the whole matter undoubtedly is, I think by pursuing it, we could well open a can of worms that would be much better left undisturbed.'

Emily gave a rude snort. 'Since when has that bothered him?'

* * *

MONDAY MORNING and the excitement of the weekend has vanished along with the warm weather. Shivering, I turn on the small heater for the first time since March. Alex and Freddy have gone on their honeymoon to Barbados, so I'm left holding the fort.

Truthfully, I could have done with his support given that the chances of my employer not having read my mother's interview are akin to her wearing two shoes the same colour - in other words, slim to none.

And assuming she *has* read it. I've no doubt she's going to want an exclusive on my side of the story.

Of course you might think that since Sebastian is her only son, and a peer of the realm to boot, she'd want to bury his connection to the daughter of a female sumo wrestler somewhere the sun doesn't shine - but you'd be completely wrong.

Daphne Sinclair – Daphers to her friends – thrives on drama. And when there isn't any, she makes it up. I've tried to tell her on numerous occasions that telling the world that Albert Doddridge is having an affair with the bingo caller at the British Legion, when she's absolutely no idea whether it's true or not, could land her in jail. She seems to find the possibility exciting – even going as far as researching open prisons in the event she finally gets through all her allowance.

Unfortunately, her son is no more exempt from her relentless search for a scoop of national proportions than the rest of us.

Walking along the river towards the cupboard that doubles as the Dartmouth Herald's office, I try out different excuses in my mind. All of which will almost certainly have as much effect as a fart in a thunderstorm.

And any forlorn hope I might have harboured that she's still oblivious to my sudden notoriety disappears as I push open the office door and come face to face with a bottle of fizz and two glasses. Heart sinking, I shut the door behind me. So far there's no sign of the dowager Duchess herself (not that we're allowed to call her that), so I can only assume she's gone out to fetch some salmon blinis to go with our Champagne – she's very fond of salmon blinis. To be fair, I'm rather partial to them myself, but it's a bit early in the day for celebratory fizz and canapés – especially when it's my private life going arse over tit that's the reason for the celebration.

I shrug off my coat and put my phone down onto the desk, just as it starts to ring. Glancing down, my heart does its usual little flip when I see Sebastian's name flash up.

'How can I help you, your grace?' I deadpan once the phone's at my ear.

'Don't tempt me,' he retorts, and I can almost hear the grin in his voice. 'Is my batty mother present?'

'Fortunately, not,' I sigh. 'But the bottle of Champagne on ice doesn't bode well for a tiny twenty-five-word article on the back page.'

He laughs out loud and all of a sudden, I feel so much better. I'm taking this whole thing far too seriously. My employer doesn't know anything about my mother's organised crime connection, all she wants are a few funny anecdotes about my childhood.

'Do you want me to put my foot down?' he asks.

I give a dry chuckle. 'Like that will do any good. Don't worry, I'll give her a few humorous, never before heard stories about growing up in Japan with a sumo wrestling, non-Japanese mother. It's not as if she knows anything about my mother's secret life of crime.'

'As long as you're sure. I'm here if you need some muscle.'

'Don't worry, I'll keep it very low key. She'll be bored within half an hour.' I cut the call and pull my laptop towards me, just as my employer breezes in through the door with a broad smile on her face, clutching a box of goodies.

'So, darling, I'd have brought two bottles of champers if I'd known beforehand that your mother worked for the *Yakuza*.'

I stare at her, wondering how long a stretch I'd get for murdering my uncle. Clearly, he'd shared my impulsive comment with Mabel. I grit my teeth. 'I'm hoping that little snippet has not been shared with the whole of your *Ladies Afloat* group?'

'Of course not darling. Naturally, I swore Mabel to secrecy. It's hardly a scoop if everybody in Dartmouth knows about it.'

'Well, she didn't work for the *Yakuza*,' I counter. 'I just think she was a person of interest a long time ago.'

'How long?' My employer hands me a glass of bubbly, and I have time to note that her eyes are actually shining. Bugger.

'When my dad and I left Japan. So, well over thirty years.' Okay, I'm exaggerating a bit, but anything that might put her off…

'Did they have a contract out on her?' Daphers knocks back her first glass and starts pouring a second. I'm beginning to feel as though I'm in the middle of the bloody *Bourne Identity*.

'Of course they didn't have a contract out on her,' I scoff, knowing nothing of the sort. 'And I've heard from her on and off through the years. It's not as if she's been in hiding.' Obviously the last two sentences are complete lies. I haven't had sight nor sound of my mother since she walked out of the door.

'There really isn't any more to this story than the paper has already printed,' I add, crossing my fingers on my lap. 'But I can give the Herald the scoop on what it was like growing up with her. I would have thought the chances of a big national picking up the story are pretty good.' I unashamedly dangle the carrot in front of her. A quick win like this will do wonders for her precious paper.

She stares at me pensively for a few seconds, sipping her fizz. Eccentric Seb's mother might be, but she's anything but stupid. And I know she's smelling a story. I'm just starting to sweat by the time she shrugs her shoulders and helps herself to a blini. 'Well, I'd better let you get on then sweetie. Obviously if you can include some funny business, that would be rather super.'

'What kind of funny business?' I ask.

'Oh, you know darling, sumo orgies, loin cloth bondage, that kind of thing.'

'How would I know about anything like that?' I protest. 'I wasn't even seven when she left. I was thinking of writing about her dedication to the profession. What it was like to be a sumo wrestling orphan. How that made me feel. No smutty stuff.'

'Smutty stuff sells newspapers, Theodora. Never forget that.' She picks up the half-drunk bottle of Champagne, pushes in the cork and slips it carefully in her bag. 'I don't want to risk stifling your creative urge sweetie. Wing me a copy of the first draft as soon as you've finished it.'

Seconds later the door slams behind her, and I'm alone.

'I THOUGHT Teddy looked very strained over the weekend,' Tory declared as she came back into the living room after putting the twins to bed.

'Hardly surprising given the curveball she was thrown about her mother,' Jason retorted. 'I'd have been bloody strained too.'

'Well, you've had enough curveballs thrown from your witch of a grandmother, God rest her soul,' Kit muttered.

Tory sat down and picked up her glass of wine. 'I just have this feeling there's more to it than she was letting on. Did you notice how she kept glancing over at Sebastian yesterday at breakfast – as though she was uncertain. And let's face it, Teddy's never uncertain about anything.'

'It was a bit peculiar,' Kit conceded. 'You think she was hiding something?'

'I do, and whatever it was, I think my father's in it up to his neck as usual.'

'I can't imagine Teddy, confiding anything to the Admiral,' Jason scoffed. 'She'd have to be barking.'

'Or pissed,' Tory said thoughtfully. 'And she was certainly well oiled when I went to bed.'

'That's not like her either,' Kit added. 'And when she was asking about the Admiral and you mentioned he'd already left, she definitely went pale.'

'Only three renditions of *The Gruffolo* tonight. I think we're getting there.' Noah entered the room after putting Isaac to bed. 'Damn, you all look serious. Did I miss anything?'

'We were talking about Teddy.' Tory handed him a glass of wine as he sat down next to her. 'Do you think she looked strained this weekend?'

'Hardly surprising, considering.' Noah's comment was almost identical to Jason's.

'Tory thinks she was hiding something,' Kit added, picking up her sparkling water with a grimace. 'God, what I wouldn't give to have some white wine in this.'

'Not long now sweetheart.' Jason placed a soft kiss on her cheek in sympathy.

Noah frowned. 'What the hell could be worse than what's already come out?' He bent forward to pick up a handful of peanuts. 'I mean every godawful picture they could lay their hands on has already been published. Teddy just has to sit it out. We all know how quickly the paparazzi move on.'

'Sebastian didn't seem bothered by it at all,' Tory conceded. 'I think Teddy was expecting him to give her the heave-ho.'

'Of course she was. She's your cousin and my friend. She's learned from the best.' Kit's voice dripped sarcasm, and Tory raised her glass with a small chuckle.

'Seb's a really good guy. And good guys don't cut and run at the first hurdle.' Noah took his wife's hand and kissed it.

'Okay, point taken,' Tory grumped. 'That's today's less-than-subtle reminder of what a numpty I was. But if there's the remotest chance my father's stuck his nose into whatever it is she's hiding, then I think I'm right to be concerned.'

'Amen,' Jason retorted drily.

'Well, we have three days to find out exactly what it is,' Kit concluded. 'There's no way I'm going back to Scotland without dragging it out of her, warts and all.'

* * *

'YOU WANT ME TO COME OVER?' I fight the urge to say yes. It would be so easy to simply lean on Sebastian. Let him ease my anxieties the way he always does. But in the end, I tell him I'm fine, that I'm intending to have an early night. It's the truth, I am, but that's not the reason I turned down his offer.

I've never been used to leaning on anyone. Sebastian is the first person I've truly let in. And believe me, that's a work in progress. Writing about my childhood in Japan today brought back more than just memories. It brought back with a vengeance the feeling that the only person I can trust to take care of me – is me. I feel as though I've stepped back to how it was when I left the NCA. For the first time in ages, the urge to up sticks and walk away swamps me.

And that's not good. I know it isn't. Not for me, or for my relation-ships. Not just with Seb. But with Tory, Kit and the others. This last year, for the first time in my life, I've been truly happy. And the last thing I want to do is to shut them out like I would have in my pre-Dartmouth days.

Naturally, I intend to have a quiet word with my uncle, but whatever his intentions, I'm certain he'll find nothing about my mother's *Yakuza* connections. I didn't, even with all the resources of the NCA behind me. Oh, I was careful. Made sure not to trigger any red flags, but by the end of my investigation, I truly believed my mother was dead – likely at the bottom of a seedy alley in Tokyo.

But then three days ago I was proved wrong.

I sit down on my brightly coloured sofa, picking at a couple of left-over blinis. Why has my mother surfaced now? And where the hell has she been all these years? Despite my initial euphoria that she made no mention of any links to organised crime, in my heart of hearts, I don't really believe she did the newspaper interview out of greed. On the face of it, speaking to the press seemed like the height of foolishness.

But what if she was doing it to alert me to the fact that she's still alive? Surely a damn letter would have been easier. But then, what if it wasn't just me she wanted to tell? The story of the duke and the sumo wrestler's daughter has gone viral. Practically the whole world knows about it. What if she instigated the initial newspaper article for protection? If anything happens to her now, it will make front page news.

My old copper's instincts kick in, and all of a sudden, I'm certain this story isn't going to simply fade away. On the contrary, whatever trouble my mother has found herself in is likely to come looking for not only me, but everyone I love. The sour taste of salmon floods my mouth and for a few seconds I fight an abrupt urge to throw up.

My gut is telling me that this is only the start…

CHAPTER 4

I wake up the next morning with the half hope that my fears of last night might seem groundless in the light of day. Unfortunately, the sense of dread doesn't seem to have lessened at all. I know I need to share my concerns with Sebastian, but the thought of bringing him more of my shit after everything he went through last year … well, I just can't do it. Not yet. Not until I have more than vague suspicions and a sick feeling of doom.

Of course, ordinarily, I would have taken my fears to Alex – since we have the same police background he'd instinctively know where I was coming from - but the last thing I want to do is disturb his honeymoon with my paranoia.

No, for the time being, this is mine to deal with. First things first. Obviously, I need to call my father. It's not beyond the realm of possibility that he actually has mum's contact details – or at least an idea of where she might have been living. We never spoke about her at all while I was growing up, and when I did my private investigation, I certainly didn't share my findings with my father. Not that there were any really, which was the main reason I believed she was dead.

All these years later, I still have no idea what her exact involvement with the *Yakuza* was. The warning to leave Japan after she disappeared told us nothing. I was always under the impression that my dad was too scared to ask.

Of course, the nature of paranoia is that it feeds on itself. How do I know my dad's phone isn't bugged? Or his house, or *mine* for that matter?

I climb into the shower, wondering if I'm completely overreacting. The chances of them getting to my or my dad's phone are pretty slim when all's said and done. And I'm making a huge assumption that my mother has something they want. Or want back. And you know what they say about assumptions?

It's more likely she did something to piss them off all those years ago and has finally either paid the debt or been forgiven.

Sighing, I turn off the shower. Organisations like the *Yakuza* don't forgive, and they don't forget. Logic tells me that whatever she did that forced her into hiding has also forced her out of it.

* * *

'You know I was there when Bill met Agnes. He was living in Nottingham then and I'd gone up for the weekend.' The Admiral shook his head. 'Seven women to every man up there, and he had to go and pick one who looked like Godzilla.'

The two men were sitting on their customary stools at the bar in the Ship Inn. 'She always had charisma though, I'll give her that,' Charles Shackleford mused thoughtfully. 'Attracted people to her – men and women. They were drawn to her for some bollocking reason.' He glanced over at Jimmy who was listening with interest. 'I used to wonder what the hell it was to be honest. I mean, she caused more fights than me and Bill put together. That was how she first got into sumo wrestling.'

'What happened?' asked Jimmy curiously.

'Put the bloody reigning champion on his back.' The Admiral chuckled. 'Bloke was in the middle of a world tour, along with about twenty other wrestlers. *Showcasing the sport*, I think they called it.' He gave another snigger. 'Old Agnes showcased him, that's for sure. Bill used to call her 'ave at 'em, Agnes when they were dating.'

'You mentioned that before, Sir.'

'The next thing I know, they've upped sticks to Japan. I was just about to join the RN, so we didn't keep in touch. Never met Teddy until that business with the Scottish strumpet.'

'How do you think she got involved with the err …' Jimmy paused and looked round the bar to check if anyone was listening before finishing with a mumbled, '*Yakuza?*'

'What are you whispering for?' the Admiral asked him irritably. 'I don't think *Oddjob's* likely to be listening behind that pot plant, do you?'

'Oh, I remember him,' Jimmy chuckled. 'I took Emily to see *Goldfinger* at the *Odeon* in Torquay.'

'Well, it's easy to see how they might have wanted to recruit someone like Agnes, but I can't even begin to think where our Bill fits into all this. He's never exactly lived life in the fast lane. He wouldn't have noticed if they'd stuck a bloody grenade underneath him.'

'Well, it seems to me, Sir, that all you have at the moment is Teddy's throw away comment when she was a little worse for wear. I mean, she might actually have been making a joke.'

The Admiral frowned, then gave a long sigh. 'You could actually be right for once, Jimmy lad. I can't believe I'm actually saying this, but on this occasion, I think it might be better if we keep an eye on things and wait and see. You fancy a packet of crisps?'

* * *

'So, come on then, spill.' Tory wastes no time in getting to the real reason for her invitation. Though she'd ostensibly arranged for me to come over and say goodbye to Kit and Jason before they headed back up to Scotland - as soon as I walk through the door, it's clear she has an ulterior motive. Clearly, the four of them have been analysing my actions over the weekend and have come to the conclusion that I'm hiding something.

I'm beginning to think I'm losing my customary poker face.

'You could at least have let me enjoy my starter,' I grumble, not bothering to argue with her.

'You can talk and eat,' Tory offers magnanimously.

I look over at the four expectant faces. It would have been six if Freddy and Alex hadn't been away. Not even Noah is giving me any wiggle room, and at length I sigh and put down my knife and fork. 'I'll need a top up,' I mutter, knocking back the rest of my glass of wine.

Tory obediently fills up my now-empty glass, and they stare at me in silent anticipation. I realise there's no way I'm leaving this room until I've divulged everything.

So finally, taking a deep breath, I tell them.

'And you told my father this,' Tory declares flatly when I eventually fall silent. They're all now regarding me as though I'm completely barking.

'Not exactly,' I protest. 'I just accidentally let it slip about her being connected to the *Yakuza*.'

'Well, you were pretty trollied,' Kit comments with a small measure of sympathy. The others just look ... well, horrified.

'I know, I know,' I groan, holding my hands in the air.

Noah purses his lips. 'To be honest, there's not really a lot the Admiral can do. He's unlikely to discover much about Japanese organised crime in Dartmouth, and at the moment, there really is no story aside from the fact that the fourteenth Duke of Blackmore is dating a sumo wrestler's daughter. With nothing to fuel it, the furore is already dying down.'

While I'd fully intended to keep my fears to myself, I abruptly find myself sharing them. When I've finally unburdened myself, I shake my head and shrug. 'I don't know whether I'm just overthinking the whole thing, but my gut is telling me that my mother's sudden desire for fame and fortune wasn't just an impulse thing.'

There's a small silence, then Jason unexpectedly takes hold of my hand. 'What Noah said still holds true. There's nothing you can do unless there are any developments.'

'Have you told Sebastian all this?' Kit asks.

'I told him about the possible *Yakuza* connection when I was worried about what she might say in the interview, but I haven't seen him since the wedding, so I haven't had the chance to tell him about my latest paranoia.'

'I don't think it's paranoia,' Tory argues. 'You were in the police force for a long time. You've always listened to your gut. Now is not the time to stop. But until something concrete happens ...' she trails off and gives a small shrug.

'Life goes on,' I mutter, raising my glass in a toast.

'Well, I hope it's all sorted before Christmas,' Kit announces, 'since I'd like all of you to spend Christmas and New Year with us in Bloodstone Tower.'

I look at her, and for once I'm absolutely speechless. Aside from the year of the Paul Ryan fiasco that led to my ignominious boot from the NCA, I've never been asked to spend the festive season with anybody.

'I...I don't know what to say,' I respond. 'That's so kind.' They all look at me like I've grown two heads.

'Don't get too excited, she's only asking because she's invited *Hello* up to take pictures of the Duke of Blackmore and Noah Westbrook enjoying Hogmanay north of the border,' Tory scoffs. 'The rest of us are totally surplus to requirements – oh, aside from babysitting duties of course...'

* * *

FOR ALL MY PANICKING, the next couple of weeks have passed quietly. Contrary to Daphers' hopes (when did I start calling her that...?) none of the nationals picked up my story. In fairness, the piece I wrote was hardly *Debbie does Dallas ...*

We're nearing the end of October now, and Christmas cards have started taking up space in the shops. The newlyweds are back, and Freddy has sprung straight into Christmas panto mode. Apparently, it's Hansel and Gretel this year and he's already been doing the unbelievably annoying, '*Oh no we don't*,' routine until I'm ready to strangle him.

Naturally, he and Alex have also been invited up to spend Christmas in Bloodstone Tower, and Freddy's already ordered a dozen kilts, but aside from briefly mentioning it to Sebastian, I've firmly put it to the back of my mind until the whole *Yakuza* problem has finally been put to bed.

Mind you, I can't actually believe how much I missed Alex while he was away. I suppose I've got used to bouncing ideas off someone, even if it's only whether printing a story about Mrs. Rodgers and her window cleaner is likely to put us in court.

Despite my conviction that there's more to the story, nothing else has so far surfaced about my mother and her supposed dodgy dealings. Though I called my dad, he had nothing new to add and said he'd never known where my mum was. In fact, I think he suspected the same as me. It had been just as much of a shock for him when he learned she was giving an interview. Truth be told, I was a little worried about him being up in Basingstoke on his own after receiving such a shock, until he told me that Delia Dawson - who's lived next door for donkey's years - was doing a perfectly good job of comforting him. I really didn't want to know what her version of *comforting* actually entailed, so I took his words at face value. Mind you, it means I won't have to worry about him over Christmas ...

Mum hasn't contacted me either, which I half thought she would. And to be honest, I don't know whether I'm relieved or not. I'm still scouring the newspapers and online for any updates, but so far, nothing. The whole story has died a death as Noah predicted it would. Fortunately, I still don't think that includes my mother.

The most positive thing to come out of the whole fiasco is Sebastian's reaction to it. He really didn't give a toss about all the negative publicity, and I love him all the more for it. I haven't yet confided my worries about my mother's reason for coming out of the woodwork when she did. We've had very little time together since the wedding and part of me thinks I should just let the whole matter go.

And today is Friday, which means Blackmore Grange's weekly *Dinner with the Duke*, so I won't be seeing him until tomorrow. Instead, while Noah's in between movies, Tory and I have established a sort of girls' night out. It might not be on a par with *Edina* and *Patsy* in *Ab Fab*, but we do our bit to give Dartmouth's gossips something to talk about. Until ten p.m. and the last ferry at least. Tonight, we're meeting in the *Dartmouth Arms*.

I'm just about to leave, when there's a knock on the door. Knowing it can only be one person, my heart sinks. If Mrs. S. thinks she's onto a good story, she's harder to get rid of than athlete's foot. In sudden inspiration, I put on my coat before answering the door. At least she'll know I'm on my way out. Not that it will stop her if she thinks she's got anything particularly juicy. Plastering a smile on my face, I throw open the door.

'Can't stop, darling,' (miracles do happen), 'but this package came for you today. I hope you don't mind, but I signed for it seeing as you weren't here.' Naturally, I don't mind, and I'm about to thank her, when she steps into the patio light, and my words die in my throat. She's wearing a full-on tiara, glinting with at least twenty diamonds. And believe me, those babies are real. Her dress is long and sparkly, though most of it is covered with a velvet dress coat that looks as though it was last worn by *Audrey Hepburn*. She's even wearing shoes the same colour. She looks quite simply magnificent – every bit the Dowager Duchess she is.

'You look wonderful,' I breathe in awe. She gives a trilling laugh.

'Thank you, sweetie. Roger's taking me to the *Angel*. I think he's going to propose.'

I blink. 'Oh … that's, that's wonderful,' I stammer, not knowing what else to say and wondering if Seb has any idea.

'Oh, it's nothing new,' she chuckles. 'He does it at least twice a year. Gives me an excuse to dress up. I shall say no, of course, like I always do.'

I have absolutely nothing to say to that, so I simply nod and smile and take the parcel from her. 'Toodle-oo,' is her parting shot as she trots back up the path.

I shake my head and look down at the package. It's small and thin, my address written in spidery writing. Stepping out into the light from the patio, I look at the postmark and my heart gives a dull thud.

It's from Japan.

Swallowing, I hesitate, wondering whether I should just leave it here, and examine it when I get back - but I know I won't be able to concentrate on anything else, and Tory will quickly smell a rat. In the end, I slip the package into my handbag and take it with me.

As per usual, I arrive first. Of course, I haven't got a set of twins under one and a toddler whose main focus in life seems to be ruining his parents' colossally expensive Persian rug. To be fair to Isaac, I'm not keen on it either…

While I'm waiting, I get us a bottle of Rosé, and a packet of crisps for Dotty – she enjoys our Friday nights too. Then I take the package out of my bag and stare down at it. Half of me is desperate to find out what's inside, but the other half is screaming at me to just get rid of it. Ordinarily, I'd wait for Tory before I started on the bottle of wine, but right now, I need the Dutch courage it might provide. Pouring myself a large glass, I take a gulp, then with trembling hands, I rip open the seal. Inside is another envelope. With a grimace of frustration, I tear it open and eventually pull out a pile of photographs.

Frowning, I hold them up towards the light. The photo on the top shows two men together. The only thing I can tell for sure is that both look oriental. I slide it down to the bottom of the pile to look at the next one, and my heart gives a sick thud. The same two men are in the photo, but standing alongside them is my mother.

'What's that you're looking at?' Tory's voice directly over my shoulder almost makes me jump out of my skin.

'Guilty conscience?' she questions, plonking herself down on the chair next to me.

I give her a droll look and wave the pile of photos at her. 'I received a package this evening. These were in it.' Suddenly reluctant to look at the rest of them, I lay the small pile down on the table and bend down to pick Dotty up, placing her in my lap where she has a bird's-eye view of the unopened packet of crisps.

Tory picks up the one on the top and squints at it as I pour her a glass of wine 'Do you know who they are?'

'No idea who the men are, but the woman is my mother.' My tone is so matter of fact that for a second Tory doesn't react, but then she turns to look at me, her eyebrows raised.

'Is it recent?'

I shrug. 'I think so. It's hard to say – I haven't seen her since I was seven.'

She puts the photo next to the pile and picks up the next one. 'I think this is your mother as well,' she comments, handing it to me, 'but I'm not sure about the men.'

I look at the photo, then turn it over. On the back is a date. I sift through to find the first one I'd looked at, then lay the three out together. 'They were taken a couple of years apart,' I murmur, picking up the next one. Sure enough, the same three people are smiling out at the camera. My mother, a man, and this time a boy around twelve or thirteen years old. There is no date on the back.

With a slightly sick feeling, I quickly go through the remaining photos. In each, all three figures appear younger. But the boy in the middle is the one who changes the most. He appears to go from adult-hood to… I pick up the last one. My much younger mother is carrying a baby. I look up at Tory who's looking at each of the pictures anxiously.

'Are you thinking what I'm thinking?' I say impassively.

She stares back at me, sympathy evident in her eyes. 'I think you have a half-brother, Teddy.'

I swallow and nod, picking the pictures back up and squinting at each of them in turn. 'I think the other man is the same in every picture, which would likely make him the father. My dad and I always thought mum had run away with a wrestler called Aki.' I pick up the picture of my mum holding the baby. 'I know it's a long time ago, but I don't remember him looking like this guy at all.'

'What are you going to do with them?'

'I've no idea. They must have come from my mother and clearly, she's telling me that she had another child after Dad and I left Japan.' I force back the ridiculous sense of betrayal that threatens to overwhelm me.

'Do you think the man in the picture could be *Yakuza?*' Tory's voice automatically goes down to a whisper, and I know she's feeling suddenly vulnerable.

'Maybe,' I state taking a fortifying drink. 'I think he might well be someone important.'

'Could he be a corrupt policeman – like in *Line of Duty?*' Tory's eyes are wide, and she glances to one side as if she expects an undercover cop to be listening from the next table. Fortunately for her peace of mind, the couple sitting at the table closest to us are at least eighty and would most likely think a *Yakuza* was a Japanese car.

I give a helpless shrug. 'We can speculate all night, but one thing is fairly certain – my mum sent them to me for two reasons. Firstly, to tell me I have a brother.

'And secondly, to keep them safe because she's afraid for her life – and possibly that of her son.'

'Well, if your mother sent them to you to keep them safe, why give an interview to the tabloids?' Tory returned to her normal level of decibels, obviously reassured by the couple's clearly visible hearing aids. 'I mean, she might as well just have given whoever's after them bloody directions to Dartmouth.'

CHAPTER 5

I'm silent for a moment, mulling over her words. Tory's absolutely right, it makes no sense for my mother to tell the world where her daughter is, then send a bunch of possibly sensitive photos for said daughter to look after.

But then, she didn't tell the world where I was. The story had already broken when my mother surfaced. Had she already sent the package? But then, how did she know I was in Dartmouth? She has to have been keeping an eye on me. That thought makes me uncomfortable on so many levels.

Or maybe she didn't know where I was until the first newspaper article?

'Do you know where the story about you and Sebastian came from?' Tory asks, clearly thinking along the same lines as me.

I give a shrug. 'If I had to guess, I'd say Seb's ex-wife, Carla. She might have been given a restraining order, but I don't think she's above making his life difficult when she can. It wouldn't have been that hard to find out about my background. I've never particularly hidden it. The NCA might not have known about my mother's possible criminal connections, but they knew about her profession. So did my school, and my so-called school friends had a bloody field day once they found out.'

Tory winces in sympathy. 'So, the NCA weren't aware of the real reason you left Japan?' she presses.

'Naturally, I kept that little gem to myself,' I respond drily, picking up my glass and taking a large sip.

Tory opens her mouth to say something more, then stops with a look of frustration on her face. 'It's no good, I've got to pee. My pelvic floor has been somewhere around my knees since Tobi and Ember were born.' I can't help it; I find myself stifling a snigger. 'You can mock all you want, sunshine,' she grumbles, climbing to her feet. 'I have an elephant's memory. Your jibes will come back to haunt you.'

'I never said a word,' I protest as she heads towards the toilet, then laugh as she holds her middle finger up behind her.

Once she's disappeared into the ladies, I pour us both another glass of wine, then lean back and sit silently for a few seconds, contemplating the different scenarios that could have led to the photographs landing on my doorstep. A small whine brings me back to the present, and I look down at Dotty who's staring at me with a world of hurt in her eyes. She's been here for over half an hour and the crisps haven't been opened yet. Chuckling, I reach for the packet and rip it open, laying a few broken ones in front of her nose.

Why the hell did my mother give the tabloid interview?

The only logical reason is the one I came up with earlier – that she wanted me to know she was alive and kicking. I only actually skim read the interview, not wanting to be dragged back into my mother's world. But I think I need to go back and read it a little more carefully. I have a sudden feeling that she might have put a clue as to her motives in the words themselves.

I look up as my cousin sits back down. 'Are you going to show the photos to Sebastian?' she demands, making her own opinion about the matter very clear.

'Of course,' I return simply. 'What good will keeping quiet about it do me? And anyway, I'm not the lone wolf I was when I first arrived in Dartmouth.'

'That you are not,' Tory grins, raising her glass to me.

'That doesn't mean I'm going to tell the world about my newly discovered family,' I continue. 'I know you'll share it with Noah, so I won't ask you not to, but the only other person besides Seb I'll take them to is Alex, and I think we might be better to keep it between the five of us while I decide what to do next.'

'Of course.' Tory nods seriously before breaking into another grin. 'Freddy will be gutted when he finds out he's missed out on being the next Jason Bourne though.'

* * *

'I REALLY DON'T KNOW why I let you talk me into these things,' Admiral Shackleford grumbled after they'd been standing next to the Jubilee Fountain in the Royal Avenue Garden for all of twenty minutes.

'It's for a good cause, Sir, and we do this every year.' He didn't add, 'and every year you moan about it,' but the inference was there. Jimmy shook his tin at a large group of what looked like students cutting through the Gardens from the Embankment.

'You'll get nothing from that direction, Jimmy lad,' the Admiral declared. 'They've got no bloody money to share for Armistice Day.' He gave a loud sigh, before adding, 'No inclination either.'

'It's not their fault,' Jimmy countered. 'They've just been brought up differently, that's all.'

'It's a changed world,' agreed the Admiral, practically sticking his tin up the nose of a large portly man who obligingly rummaged around his pockets for some loose change.

'And nobody carries any cash with them anymore,' Jimmy commented when the man had moved on.

The two men stood in silence for a few minutes. 'It won't be the same at the Cenotaph without old Boris there,' Jimmy declared sadly at length.

The Admiral grunted his agreement. 'Not to mention the fact that the service is likely to be twice as long without Boris's anal acoustics to chivvy the proceedings along.'

Jimmy gave a low chuckle. 'He certainly livened things up a bit.'

The Admiral looked at his watch. 'I reckon another half an hour and we'll have earned a pint.'

'Our stint finishes at one, Sir. We can't leave our post until then.'

'Bloody hell, Jimmy, I already need to use the toilet. Another half an hour and my back teeth'll be floating.'

'Well, it's not very busy at the moment, I can hold the fort if you want to pop over and ease springs now.'

The Admiral grimaced. 'I think that might be wise, lad, now I've started talking about it. Keep an eye on Pickles, he'll be desperate to follow me.' The spaniel gave a slight wag of his tail from his bed under their small table as he heard the sound of his name, but otherwise looked the very opposite of desperate as his master hurried across the park in the direction of the public toilets.

There was no queue, so it was only a couple of minutes before he was on his way back. As he went past the bandstand, he caught sight of a smallish, dark-haired man wearing all black. He was looking down at his phone, turning it this way and that. The Admiral couldn't have said what it was about the figure that caught his attention, but seconds later, when the man looked up, his heart did a double flip. Charles Shackleford would have bet his prize medals that the fellow was Japanese.

Without thinking, the Admiral stepped behind a bush. The fact that there happened to be a Japanese man in Dartmouth really wasn't anything to get excited about – the area certainly had its fair share of tourists from that part of the world, but something about this fellow looked shifty. When the man began walking towards the town, Charles Shackleford hesitated only briefly before following.

A few seconds later he passed Jimmy, who was fortunately preoccupied with a couple of former comrades in arms who'd brought the troops a couple of fortifying pasties. The Admiral's steps faltered slightly at the tantalising aroma, but seconds later, he stiffened his spine. If there was any skulduggery afoot, it was his job to ferret it out. Sadly, it also meant that Pickles would very likely end up with his pasty – especially as the spaniel's attention was focussed entirely on the steaming paper bag sitting on the table.

Sighing, Admiral Shackleford hurried after his quarry who'd already left the park and was about to head up Duke Street.

After initially looking uncertain, the small man was now striding confidently along the pavement. The Admiral hoped he wasn't going all the way to the top of Victoria Road - the last stretch would challenge a bloody mountain goat.

Fortunately, after only a hundred yards, the man turned left into Anzac Street. Wondering if he could be heading to the Dartmouth Herald's office, the Admiral broke into a trot to catch up and turned the corner in time to see the man stride past the church. Seconds later, the fellow turned left into Smith Street. Putting a bit of a spurt on, Charles Shackleford finally staggered out onto Smith Street, just in time to see his quarry open the door to the *Seven Stars* pub. What the bloody hell was he going into Dartmouth's oldest pub for? He'd stick out like a tomato in a fruit salad.

The Admiral looked back the way he'd come, now seriously bemoaning his missed Cornish pasty, until a sudden thought crossed his mind. He might have time for a quick pint while he was keeping an eye on Nick Nack. With renewed enthusiasm, he hurried towards the pub entrance and seconds later was blinking inside the doorway, waiting for his eyes to adjust to the dimness.

An initial sweep of the room failed to reveal anyone of oriental persuasion, and since the interior really wasn't very big, the small man appeared to have disappeared into thin air. Frowning, the Admiral stepped away from the door. The pub had already started filling up with the Saturday lunchtime crowd, but he was able to reach the bar easily enough. Once there, he gave the room another scan, and finally spotted his quarry sitting at a small table round the side of the bar. Incongruously, he was sipping on a pint of real ale and nibbling on a packet of cheese and onion crisps. He also appeared to be reading what looked like a thin broadsheet.

Ordering himself a pint, Charles Shackleford debated his next move. On the face of it, the man didn't appear to be doing anything suspect. He could simply be a real ale fanatic. The Admiral sneaked a quick glance. From this angle, he couldn't quite see what the fellow was reading. Did it matter? He had absolutely nothing to go on besides a hunch, and though he would never have admitted it – even to Jimmy - his so-called intuition had got him in hot water more times than he could remember.

Even so, he couldn't just call it a day without turning over every stone. Taking a deep breath, he stood up and walked over to the table. 'You look a long way from home, Sir,' he observed jovially.

The stranger looked up, his initial irritation quickly hidden behind a mask of politeness. He stood up and gave a slight bow. 'You are correct,' he returned, his English excellent despite a slight accent, 'I am on vacation in your wonderful country.' His use of the word *vacation* had the Admiral wondering if he'd learned his English in America.

'I see you like real ale,' Charles Shackleford continued genially, while unobtrusively trying to get a look at the man's reading matter. 'A man after my own heart. Have you tried Devon Dumpling?'

There was a small silence, and the Admiral could tell the fellow was wondering how to get rid of him without causing a scene. Good luck to him. Finer men than Nick Nack here had tried. He stood his ground, an inane grin on his face.

'Is that what you are drinking?' the man finally asked through gritted teeth.

Admiral Shackleford gave an enthusiastic nod and seated himself at the small table, leaving his newfound friend no well-mannered alternative but to sit back down himself.

'Jimmy Noon at your service.' The Admiral offered up his best friend's name without so much as a qualm.

The man's lips turned up in the vaguest approximation of a polite smile, but he didn't offer his own name. Instead, he waved down at the broadsheet on the table in front of him. 'I was attempting to read your local newspaper,' he explained.

'That's impressive,' Charles Shackleford enthused. 'I reckon your English is a lot better than my Chinese.'

'I am from Japan,' the man retorted stiffly. 'Perhaps you can help me. My English is not so good to understand some of this article. Could you read it to me?'

The Admiral's brief feeling of triumph at being right about the fellow's nationality turned to dust as the man held out a copy Dartmouth Herald. The article he'd been reading was about Teddy.

* * *

I LOVE SATURDAYS. Seb and I have got into the habit of spending the weekends together whenever possible, and the anticipation of spending two whole days with him still makes me feel all gooey inside. Naturally the old me would have run in the opposite direction as fast and as far as possible, but that Teddy has well and truly gone. I might still be prickly and opinionated, but I'm no longer emotionally repressed. Well, not *that* much anyway.

I haven't had the chance to re-examine my mother's newspaper interview, but since I fully intend to show the photographs to Sebastian, I thought maybe we could go over it together. It's my turn to go over to Blackmore, and since I still haven't got a car, my beloved is sending over his – just one of the little perks of dating a duke …

While I'm waiting for Seb's chauffeur, Jamie, to arrive, I send a quick message to Tory reminding her not to tell anyone other than Noah about the pictures. The sense of unease I've felt since my mother surfaced is slowly morphing into full blown paranoia. If my mother sent the photos to me because she was afraid they'd fall into the wrong hands, those wrong hands could very well want them badly. I really don't like the idea of my friends caught up in some kind of oriental gangland feud, and I'm not foolish enough to believe that the *Yakuza's* arms are not long enough to reach the UK.

I would take them to the NCA if I had anything other than hunches. So far, no crime has been committed, and my ex-colleagues would doubtless tell me to come back when I had a dead body. Not to mention the fact that while my mother really isn't my favourite person, I would prefer not to endanger her or my possible half-sibling by taking the pictures to the authorities. At least until I've worked out what the bloody hell is going on.

I'm well aware that my selflessness has not extended to keeping Sebastian out of the murky picture. But common sense tells me the Yakuza would be reluctant to cause any harm to someone high up in the echelons of British society without good reason. The rest of us are unimportant little people and completely disposable.

A sudden ping on my phone brings me out of my reverie, and looking down, see the thumbs-up emoji followed by a kiss. I know that Tory will do as I ask. Being the Admiral's daughter, she's seen first-hand on numerous occasions the devastating effects of going rogue. Not that she won't insist on being kept in the loop. She's not stupid, but she *is* nosy.

A knock on my door tells me my ride has arrived. No matter how much I tell Jamie that he doesn't need to actually collect me from my doorstep, he still insists on escorting me to the car.

Forty-five minutes later, we're driving through the gates leading to Blackmore Grange. The first sight of the house still gives me the feeling of being in a *Disney* fairytale. And at the end of the day, that's what my relationship with Sebastian is. I'm well aware that the chances of us staying together until we're old and grey are very slim. I'm hardly Duchess – or even marriage – material. But so far, we've successfully kept the whole subject of the *future* out of our time together.

As I get out of the car, the gate to the rose garden opens, and I feel the usual warm and fuzzy knowing that Seb has obviously been watching for my arrival. He's not the only one. I laugh as a whirlwind of black and white fur comes charging across the stable courtyard towards me. I crouch down and open my arms just in time for Coco to throw herself into them. After a minute or so, I push her away and climb to my feet, waving at Jamie, who is already returning the car to the garage.

The sight of Sebastian leaning against the gatepost, a lazy smile of welcome on his beautiful face, turns my insides to liquid. My heartbeat quickens as he pushes himself away from the post and walks towards me. Seconds later, it's my turn to be enfolded, and Seb takes his time telling me how pleased he is to see me – a sentiment I enthusiastically return. When we finally break apart, he takes my overnight bag but keeps one arm around my shoulders until we separate to walk through the gate leading to his private quarters.

'I thought we'd have lunch on the balcony while the sun's out.' He opens the door and stands aside to let me through – all impeccable manners, as usual. 'I have blankets, of course.'

'That would be lovely,' I smile, leaning in to give him a quick peck as I pass. Seconds later, we're in his sumptuous penthouse, and I finally relax. This, and my little shed in Dartmouth, are our boltholes.

'I asked for lunch at one,' he murmurs, pulling me to him. That gives us an hour …

CHAPTER 6

*H*eart thudding, the Admiral gave a small, self-conscious cough and looked down at the article. It had been written by Teddy herself and described her life growing up in Japan as the daughter of a well-known sumo wrestler or *Rikishi* as they are apparently known.

Slowly, he read the article aloud, occasionally looking up to see his companion's reaction. As soon as he'd finished, he folded up the newspaper and laid it on the table. The man said nothing for a moment, then abruptly he sneered, revealing a mouth full of gold teeth.

'She is no *Rikishi*. Women cannot be in the ring. She is foolish *Yariman* who does not know her place.' The sheer venom in his outburst was completely unexpected, and the Admiral was suddenly overcome with panic. He had no idea what a *Yariman* was, but clearly it wasn't very complimentary.

'Well, I don't know about that,' he bluffed, 'but it doesn't look as though the lass who wrote the article ever sees her mother.' He paused for a second, then added, 'Are you from a newspaper yourself?'

The man stared at him with narrowed eyes for a second, then finishing his crisps and drink, fastidiously wiped his fingers with his napkin and stood up. 'My thanks for your assistance,' he said brusquely. Aside from a slight bow, he'd abandoned all semblance of politeness. 'I must go.' Then, picking up the Herald, he turned and walked away. To the Admiral's surprise, he didn't head towards the exit, but to the set of stairs opposite the bar. Evidently, Nick Nack was staying in the pub.

The Admiral quickly downed the rest of his pint and hurried outside to retrace his steps. Jimmy would be wondering what the bloody hell had happened to him.

'Sir, I was beginning to get worried,' the small man exclaimed when he finally arrived back at their position in the park. 'Are you all right?'

The genuine fear in the small man's eyes took the Admiral a little aback, and he realised in that moment just how lucky he was to have a friend like Jimmy Noon. An unfamiliar sense of gratitude flooded him for a few seconds, along with the bizarre notion to give his friend a quick hug. Naturally, both sentiments vanished a few seconds later and the only indication he'd felt anything untoward was a slight gruffness in his voice. 'You'll never guess what I've been up to, Jimmy, lad.'

'I can't even begin to imagine, Sir.' The Admiral regarded his so-called friend irritably, any lingering gratefulness disappearing quicker than you could say *kumbaya*.

After a couple of seconds, however, the elation over what he'd discovered replaced his annoyance, and he related the events of the last forty-five minutes. 'So, I was right, the *Yakuza* are here looking for Teddy,' he finished triumphantly a few minutes later.

Jimmy was silent for a moment as he took in his former superior's words. 'Well, I think you should definitely warn Teddy that a Japanese person was interested in an article she wrote,' he said at length.

'He wasn't just interested in the article,' the Admiral countered, 'the bloke knew Agnes. Called her a *yarim*... something. No idea what it means, but it's obvious they don't exchange Christmas cards.'

'That might well be, Sir, but it doesn't mean he's a member of the *Yakuza*. And he's done nothing illegal – that we're aware of anyway.'

'What about his gold teeth?' the Admiral argued.

'Lots of people have gold teeth,' Jimmy retorted, trying desperately to stem the Admiral's customary investigative fervour.

Charles Shackleford was silent for a moment, and Jimmy stared at him in sudden trepidation. He knew that look of old. Seconds later, the small man's fear was realised.

'Just because we don't know what he's been up to, doesn't mean he's not been up to no good. For all we know, he could have offed half of bloody Dartmouth. And he's definitely got it in for old Teddy.' He rummaged around in his pocket and brought out a screwed-up napkin. 'Time for you to earn your crust, Pickles.' The spaniel looked up and wagged his tail.

Jimmy frowned at the tissue, then looked at the Admiral. 'We're just going to have to find the evidence to incriminate the bastard,' Charles Shackleford declared enthusiastically. 'By the way, is there any of that pasty left over?'

* * *

'So, you think the man in the picture is - or was – your mother's paramour when you and your dad left Japan?' Sebastian queries. 'Have you any idea who he was?'

I shake my head. 'But I think it's pretty clear that the boy in between them is their son, and therefore, my half-brother.'

'She's certainly waited a long time before letting you in on her secret.

There has to be a bloody good reason why she's sent these to you now.'

I sigh in agreement. 'Could it be as a result of the newspaper coverage do you think, or something else?'

We're still sitting outside on the balcony, though I suspect we'll be heading back inside shortly as the sun begins to lose its autumn warmth. I pull my blanket tighter around my shoulders and snuggle into his heat.

'I can't imagine your sudden publicity would have been the catalyst to inform you that you have a half-brother,' Sebastian says thoughtfully. 'Or not the only thing at least. If anything, I'd have thought that seeing you suddenly being plastered all over the tabloids would have made her hunker down until the furore had passed.'

'Unless my sudden meteoric rise to fame came at just the right time.' I lean forward to pick up the photos. 'What do these pictures say?' I lay them out in order on the table. 'If nothing else, they prove fairly conclusively that she had a son with whoever the man is in the photo.'

I look over at Sebastian with a frown. 'I think for some reason she now needs the world to know it...'

'...Because both their lives are for some reason at risk.' Sebastian finishes looking down at me seriously. 'If that's the case, sweetheart, she's put you, her only daughter in the same danger.'

'Well, she was never strong on the maternal front - where I was concerned anyway,' I mutter drily. 'But why do the interview with the press? She didn't mention anything at all about a son or having another relationship after my father.'

'Perhaps she was trying to tell you something.' Sebastian echoes my earlier thoughts, and I look over at him with a grin.

'I knew there was a reason why I fell in love with you.'

'So, it wasn't for my good looks and sparkling personality?'

'Those too.' I favour him with my approximation of a lascivious wink, and he winces.

'You might well be the sexiest woman I've ever met,' he grins back at me, 'but when you do that, you look like *Benny Hill*.'

I fake a hurt look. 'Fortunately for you, my brain is better than my seduction techniques.' I lean to the side and grab my handbag, pulling out two sheets of A4 paper. 'I printed a couple of copies of mum's interview for us to go through.'

'Mmm, old school. Very Phillip Marlowe.'

'I've found that nothing replaces a paper and pen when you're looking for something specific,' I explain, handing him a copy.

'Shall we take them inside?' he suggests. 'I think your nose might be turning blue.'

I give a fervent nod, throwing off my blanket and leaning to lift up a corner of the pile of blankets next to me. 'You can come out now, sweetie, Daddy's letting us inside.'

Seb gives me a droll look as Coco sticks her head out of her cocoon. 'You have no romance in your soul,' he grumbles, grabbing his laptop and getting to his feet.

'I'm an ex-copper, what did you expect?' I shoot back, gathering the rest of our stuff and following him into the blessedly warm living area.

Five minutes later, we're ensconced on the sofa, and I pick up the copy of my mother's interview.

On first scan, there doesn't appear to be anything in it of any particular note. The article is mainly humorous anecdotes of her brief time in the ring, but she does express her regret at leaving me. *Aww, bless.*

Ignoring the hurt that even all these years later threatens to grab me by the throat, I begin to concentrate on the small print. There is one story that seems a little out of context because it's the only one that mentions her arrival in Japan. She talks about being introduced to a man who told her his grandfather was once a member of the Japanese Imperial family.

* * *

'How on earth are you going to get access to his room?' Jimmy stared at his former superior in exasperation.

They'd finished their charity stint for the British Legion and were now back having a drink at the *Ship*.

'I'm not, Mabel is,' the Admiral retorted, taking a sip of his pint. The large man's complacent nod chilled Jimmy to the core.

'So, you're willing to let your fiancée do the breaking and entering?'

'She won't be breaking and entering, she'll be cleaning.'

'Mabel isn't a cleaner, Sir.'

The Admiral scowled over at his companion. 'I *know* she's not a cleaner, Jimmy, but she will be by tomorrow.'

'Is she taking a crash course in domestic management?'

The Admiral gave a pained sigh. 'They're looking for cleaners over at the Seven Stars, so I thought Mabel could pop over for an interview.'

'Have you asked her?'

'Get a bloody grip Jimmy. How could I have asked her? I've been with you all day.'

'You can't just arrange this behind her back, Sir.'

'Why not. It's for a good cause. Mabel's very fond of Teddy.'

Jimmy opened his mouth to utter another protest, then shut it again.

He was wasting his breath. Hopefully, Mabel would refuse and that would be the end of it.

'If it goes according to plan, she'll be starting her first shift on Monday. And then, Jimmy lad, we'll nail the blighter.'

'You just can't leave Mabel to search his room,' Jimmy argued, his voice rising, much to the interest of those around them. Fortunately, at this time of day, the pub was very quiet.

'No need to shout,' the Admiral hissed. 'I was thinking I'd be the one doing the searching. All Mabel needs to do is let me in. Nick Nack won't be any the wiser.'

'Who's Nick Nack?' Jimmy asked, now completely bewildered.

The Admiral sighed. 'Keep up, Jimmy. You're like a bloody fart in a trance. *The Man with the Golden Gun* – you know, the side kick of that bloke who usually has fangs.'

'Oh, you mean Scaramanga,' Jimmy nodded. 'That was Christopher Lee. I don't think he had fangs in that film, but he did have three nipples.'

'What did he do with the third one when they finished filming?' Charles Shackleford asked, interested despite himself.

'Oh, I don't think they were real...' Jimmy paused and thought for a second. 'Well, at least one of them wasn't.'

There was a short silence, then Jimmy added, 'I don't think Nick Nack was from Japan.'

'He told me he was.'

'When did he tell you that?'

'When I chatted with him.'

'You never mentioned you'd spoken to him – when was that, Sir? Did you meet Christopher Lee too?'

'I met Christopher Lee once.' Both men turned to look at Bernard, a fellow regular who was nursing a pint at the nearest table. 'If I'm being honest, I was a bit disappointed. Offered him the missus, but when he'd finished with her, she didn't burst into flames – not even when I took her to Torquay. Bloody waste of money it was…'

CHAPTER 7

'I didn't realise my mother was introduced to Japanese Royalty when we first arrived in Japan.' I turn to Sebastian with a frown. 'As far as I'm aware, the fact that she was a woman and a foreigner to boot made her pretty much persona non grata with the sumo wrestling purists.'

Sebastian doesn't answer for a second as he re-reads the story my mother related about her meeting, then he looks over at me. 'She says this man's grandfather *was* a member of the Imperial family. I can only assume that means his grandfather was dead at the time of their meeting.'

I have a sudden thought. 'Didn't the Japanese Emperor step down a few years ago?'

Sebastian nods. 'In 2019. The current Emperor is his son, Naruhito.'

I lean back against the sofa. 'When I was at school in Tokyo, we never spoke the Emperor's name at all – I seem to remember it was considered impolite. I think it's only in the West that his name is actually used, and then it's only ever the first name. I remember being baffled by it all.' I shrug and add, 'All very interesting but not particularly useful.'

'Well, I think we can safely say that whoever the man your mother refers to actually was, his meeting with an upstart foreign female sumo wrestler had nothing to do with the Emperor.'

I sit chewing on my lip for a few moments, then I pick up the photo showing my mother holding the baby. 'There's no date on this photo, but it can't have been that long after she did her runner.' I hold the picture closer. 'The man she's with looks roughly the same age as her...' I trail off and grab hold of Sebastian's arm. 'What if the man in this photo is the man she met when we first arrived in Japan - the man who claimed his grandfather was a member of the Imperial family?'

'It makes sense,' Sebastian concedes, taking the photo from me. 'Do you think they could have married?'

'As far as I'm aware, she never divorced my father, and anyway, I doubt very much that a member of the Imperial Japanese family, however far removed, would tie himself legally to a gaijin.' At his enquiring look, I add, 'Westerner.'

'So, you think he could have set her up as his mistress?' I grin at the antiquated term.

'Bloody hell, my mother - a *concubine* of Japanese royalty, even if it is only a distant cousin. Now there's a turn up for the books.'

Sebastian shakes his head, more than a little bemused. 'I think I need a drink,' is all he comments drily, climbing to his feet. 'Red okay?' I nod absently, my mind still preoccupied with my mother's convoluted past.

When my mother left, the *Yakuza* turned up almost immediately, looking for something and warning my father to leave Japan. Was this man the key? I stroke Coco's soft fur absently, allowing my mind to do its thing. The pictures in my possession suggest they had a son together. A son that is now an adult. I pick up the photo, showing only the two men, as Seb returns with the wine. Taking a sip, I turn the photo over and look at the date. The picture was taken two years ago, and I'd estimate the son to be in his late twenties at the time.

What are we missing? Clearly the identity of the man is important. My mother wouldn't have sent his picture had he been irrelevant. My mind feels as though it's dancing on the edge of something, but experience tells me I can't force it. All I can do is wait. Until eventually whatever it is hits me like a runaway train ...

* * *

'I'M REALLY NOT VERY sure about this, Charlie. I mean, I love a good spring clean as much as the next person, but I don't really want to get involved with a bunch of Chinese spies.'

The Admiral gritted his teeth, before saying in his most soothing tone, 'You won't, my dove. And there'll be no spring cleaning, just a quick dust round before you open the door and let me in. You'll hand in your notice the same day.'

The matron pursed her lips, and the Admiral's heart sank. Mabel might not be the sharpest knife in the drawer, but when she had a bit of a wendy on, there was no shifting her. Still, before he gave up on his plan entirely, he had one last tactic up his sleeve. 'Mabel, my angel, we need to find some kind of evidence against this varmint, so we can take it to the police.' This time he used his most wheedling tone, the one he put on when he wanted her to make him a steak and kidney pudding.

She was silent for a moment, and the Admiral schooled his features into anxious and concerned. Seconds later, she gave an abrupt nod, and Charles Shackleford resisted the impulse to swing her round in the air as it would undoubtedly put his back out.

'Right then, get your best kit on for nine a.m. tomorrow and we'll be on the ten past ferry.'

'What time is the interview?' Mabel asked, clearly still a bit apprehensive.

'Eleven thirty. I tell you what, I'll treat you to some fish and chips afterwards, and we'll eat them on the Embankment, just like we did when we first met.'

'The last time I had an interview was up at the Naval College,' she mused. 'My, I had a good time while I worked there. All those handsome young men.'

The Admiral frowned, assailed by an unaccustomed jealousy. 'I didn't know you worked up there,' he commented gruffly. 'You weren't there during my time.'

'Now that's where you're wrong, Charlie Shackleford, but I had other fish to fry then.' She winked and climbed to her feet with a small chuckle. 'Best to let sleeping dogs lie.'

The Admiral stared at her like she'd just grown another head. Mabel rarely talked about her younger life, and he thought it was because she'd been unhappy. But obviously, it hadn't all been unrelenting misery …

* * *

Sebastian lay in bed, listening to Teddy's soft breathing next to him and Coco's from the bottom. They were practically in sync, and he smiled to himself in the dark. They'd come to bed over two hours ago and their lovemaking had been intense, almost violent. Instinctively sensing that Teddy needed his body to crush her fears about her mother, he'd responded to her urgency and given her exactly what she needed. At the end, as he'd listened to her cries and felt her shudder and clench around him, his release had been so powerful, it almost felt as though he was pouring his soul into her rather than just his seed.

Sometimes it scared him how quickly Teddy Shackleford had wheedled her way into his heart. After his marriage to Carla had gone south, he truly believed he'd never get married again. But more than that; he'd been absolutely determined he'd never allow another woman into his life.

And then Teddy had come along and completely turned it upside down. She was different in every way to his first wife. It wasn't that loving her was easy. She was impatient and defensive, and fiercely independent. Outward shows of affection didn't come naturally to her, and it was only when they'd visited the South of France to stay with Tory and Noah while the actor was on location that she'd relaxed enough to even admit their relationship to people.

But what had become apparent in recent months was her clear expectation that their relationship wouldn't last. She never actually came out and said it, but it was there, in the background. He didn't know whether it was because of his title, his looks, or his money – or a combination of all three. It could be because she herself wasn't comfortable with the idea of being with someone forever. To his knowledge, she'd never had a boyfriend before – had never even considered having one. Her career had always come first - until it had gone down in flames. Their relationship had come as a surprise to both of them.

He knew she'd never given a second's thought to the idea of marrying him, and for the first few months, that suited him perfectly. But lately, his aversion to the idea had inexplicably waned. The truth was, he wanted her with him. Permanently. If he asked her to move in with him at Blackmore, she might well consider it, but if he asked her to marry him, she'd laugh him out of the room. And then she'd end their relationship immediately.

And now, with the revelations about her mother surfacing, he could feel her withdrawing. She might have come to him for help, but he sensed it wasn't because she loved him.

It was because she respected his judgement, and the pragmatic part of her knew he was the right man for the job. He was simply the logical choice. She would most likely be picking Alex's brains too first thing on Monday.

He gave an internal sigh. He loved her matter-of-factness, her ability to cut through the crap. But that same pragmatism would prevent her from saying yes to any proposal.

In Teddy's world, Dukes didn't marry sumo wrestlers' daughters.

WAKING up in Blackmore is always such a pleasure, and this morning is no exception, even after discovering my mother could well be a royal concubine. Turning over, I realise that both Seb and Coco are missing. Clearly Coco's been taken down to do her business.

Sighing, I stretch out, feeling Sebastian's fading warmth which takes me back to last night and our lovemaking. Immediately, I feel my whole body tighten. Seb really is the most incredible lover. Not that I've got much experience to draw on, but the mind-blowing sensations he creates with a mere touch... well, let's just say I've never felt anything like it before.

The subject of my thoughts chooses that moment to walk into the room, looking particularly yummy in just his pyjama bottoms. He's carrying a tray with a selection of croissants and a pot of tea. Did I mention he's house-trained too?

He puts the tray down on the small dressing table in the corner, just as Coco shoots past him to take a flying leap onto the bed. Her wet muzzle indicates she's just finished her breakfast, but that doesn't stop her from giving my pastry her undivided attention.

'You'll have to wait, sweetie,' I tell her with my mouth full as Sebastian climbs back into bed. 'Whatever your chef wants, give it to him.' I groan at length, picking up my second croissant. 'These are to die for.'

'Literally, if you eat too many,' Seb comments drily. 'I think the sugar alone might just send you into a coma.'

'Good job I don't live here all the time then,' I quip. To my surprise, there's a small silence and I look over at him, expecting to see a sardonic grin on his face. Instead, he seems closed, his face unreadable. My heart gives a dull thud. Dear God, not now. Surely, he can't be thinking of ending us now. No matter how much I've told myself that our relationship can only be temporary, I don't think I can take it on top of everything else. Which is why I feel like I've fallen down the rabbit hole at his next words.

'Would you like to move in?'

For some inexplicable reason my face goes the colour of a ripe tomato as we stare at each other. My head is telling me that he's just saying this because he's concerned about murderous Japanese gangsters leaving my broken body in an alley somewhere.

'You don't have to be worried about me,' I manage to respond at length, hating the huskiness of my voice. 'I won't do anything stupid.'

He doesn't answer. Instead, my eyes are drawn to a pulse in his neck, and I suddenly realise that unbelievably, the look on his face is nervousness. My dim-witted brain, entirely unused to dealing with messy emotions, abruptly recognises that he actually *wants* me to move in with him. Here. In Blackmore. His ancestral home.

I open my mouth, then close it again. I have no idea what to say. The desperate desire to shout, '*Yes*,' and throw myself into his arms is terrifying. In the end, I chicken out and quip, 'Ask me again after this bloody mess with my mother gets sorted and you're not just feeling sorry for me.'

He stares at me for a moment longer, and for a second, I think he's going to say something more, but finally, he just gives a twisted smile and bends forward to kiss me lightly. So why do I feel like crying?

'What are we doing today?' I ask, my voice bright, desperately trying to get back to how we'd been not five minutes ago.

Thankfully, he plays along. 'It's not raining, so I thought we'd take Coco and walk down to the River. It's about four miles. Can your city legs cope with that?'

'Is that four miles in total, or each way?' I deadpan.

He raises his eyebrows. 'Each way of course.'

'And how many hills?' This time he just grins at me. Yep, we're looking at south Devon's answer to Mount Everest. 'Bring it on,' I declare defiantly, throwing back the covers. 'But you'd better be taking a bloody picnic.'

* * *

'Do you think Teddy will mind if I tell Kit about the photos?'

'I think you're missing the point a little, honey. It's not whether she minds, she's afraid that whoever knows about them could well be in danger. To be honest, I think we really need to butt out of this one. Leave it to Teddy to fix. She's the expert.'

They were taking a leisurely stroll along the Embankment, enjoying the late autumn sunshine before heading to the Bayard's Cove Inn for a Sunday roast lunch. The twins were fast asleep in their double buggy, and Isaac was skipping along in front, trying to keep up with a large yacht skimming through the water.

Keeping her eyes firmly on their son, Tory pulled a face before sighing. 'I know you're right. I just can't seem to help myself. I'm coming to the conclusion that excessive curiosity is a Shackleford failing. I suppose we should be grateful that my father hasn't embroiled himself in the whole thing.'

'How do we know he hasn't?' Noah countered.

Tory frowned. 'He and Jimmy were doing their annual British Legion poppy selling yesterday, so that would have kept him out of mischief, and when I went over to see him on Thursday, he didn't have that shifty look he gets when he's up to no good. I can always tell when he's doing something he shouldn't.'

They reached the upper ferry, and Tory took hold of Isaac's hand to let him watch the cars disembark. They were just about to cross the road to give the little boy some play time on the park, when she suddenly spotted the subject of their discussion making his way down the ramp, Mabel at his side. 'Speak of the devil,' she murmured to Noah, nodding towards the couple.

'Mabel looks very smart,' Noah commented as Isaac caught sight of his grandparents and started waving excitedly.

'Dad doesn't look exactly happy to see us,' Tory frowned.

'Does he ever?' Noah laughed down at her.

'No, not really,' Tory conceded, 'but Mabel usually does.'

'She looks like she's been caught with her fingers in the cookie jar,' Noah agreed. 'Are we waiting to speak with them?'

Tory gave a small grimace. 'I think we need to. It's not often we catch Mabel looking shifty, and if my father has dragged her into one of his little schemes, we might be able to nip it in the bud.'

'This should be fun,' Noah murmured as the elderly couple came towards them.

'What are you doing here?' the Admiral questioned brusquely as Mabel made a fuss of Isaac.

'Hi, Dad, it's good to see you too,' Tory responded drily, well aware that her sarcasm would go straight over her father's head. 'Have you and Mabel come over for lunch?'

'Yes, we have, haven't we, Charlie?' Mabel clearly hadn't quite mastered the art of slippery and evasive that was second nature to her fiancé.

Said fiancé threw her an ill-tempered look before saying, 'We're having fish and chips. Don't let us keep you.'

Tory narrowed her eyes in suspicion before giving an exaggerated shrug. 'We're in no hurry, Dad. We can walk back into town together. Where are you getting your fish and chips from – Rockfish?'

Her father's, 'No,' at the same time as Mabel's, 'Yes,' completely sealed it. They were both up to something. Tory raised her eyebrows and waited, unmoving. Mabel hadn't got her father's brazenness, and if they stood there long enough, she'd crack. Unfortunately, just as Mabel opened her mouth to speak, a loud yell rent the air.

The Admiral didn't hesitate to use the distraction, grasping Mabel's arm and saying, 'Don't mind us, you see to little … err … what's her face. We'll leave you to it.' And with that, they both turned and hurried along the Embankment towards the town.

Tory glowered after them as Noah replaced Ember's lost dummy. 'They're definitely up to something,' she declared as the wailing abruptly subsided.

'Of that I have no doubt,' her husband chuckled, straightening. 'But I don't think you need to worry too much, darling. I doubt even your old man would be reckless enough to drag his fiancée into a possible Japanese gang war.'

CHAPTER 8

On occasion, dating someone with both a title and a Michelin starred hotel can be a little surreal. And this is one of those occasions.

It takes us over two hours to get to the River Dart and while the terrain isn't quite Mount Everest, it's hilly enough to have me wondering whether I'll be needing oxygen by the time we reach our destination.

But as we crest the last hill and I stare out over the beautiful undulating patchwork of hills, backed by the brooding peaks of Dartmoor in the distance, I'm overcome by more than a shortness of breath.

'Amazing isn't it?' I just nod, not wanting to sully the peace with conversation. Even Coco pants quietly as she flops down at my side.

In complete understanding, Sebastian takes my hand to guide me down a small trail. Five minutes later, the river finally reveals itself. And there, in the centre of a sheltered glade leading right into the water, is an actual picnic table and two chairs, complete with a white cloth, napkins and wine glasses. Oh, and a waiter. Don't forget the waiter.

'Welcome, your grace. Would either you or Ms Shackleford like an apéritif before lunch?' His voice is pure Downton Abbey, and I have to suppress the urge to clap. I look over at Sebastian in delight. He gives me a boyish grin and asks if I would like a glass of Champagne before lunch.

'That would be very agreeable, your grace,' I respond, performing a small curtsy. He laughs and shakes his head before turning back to our waiter.

'We'll have our drinks on that rock over there, Anton.'

'Very well, your grace, I'll cover it with the blanket.'

'Please tell me that's not his real name,' I whisper as Sebastian puts his hand under my elbow and guides me to a large, conveniently flat rock sticking out into the water.

'I've heard some of the staff call him Tony, and when he forgets himself, his accent is pure Manchester,' Seb grins, 'so I think it's more likely Anthony. To me, he's always been Anton.'

We seat ourselves on the luxurious wool blanket, just as *Anton* brings us both a glass of fizz.

'Would you like a wrap, Ms Shackleford? It's a little breezy this close to the water.' I shake my head and smile, not trusting myself to actually speak.

Drawing up my legs, I watch Coco as she investigates the area, her nose to the ground, before finally settling close to where the action was going to be and gazing adoringly up at Anton.

'How on earth did you get everything down here?' I ask, waving at the beautifully set table complete with silver cutlery and crystal glasses.

'A four-by -four,' Sebastian confesses. 'There's a track about two hundred yards away. I have an agreement with the farmer.'

'You do this often then?' I quip, only half joking. The thought of him bringing another woman to this magical place fills me with an unexpected jealousy.

'You're the first,' he responds quietly, and I look at him in surprise.

'Not even Carla?'

He gives me a droll look. 'Most definitely not Carla.'

I laugh, and for the next few minutes, we sit in companionable silence, watching as Anton bustles around the table, laying out various small dishes in the centre, his every move watched vigilantly by Coco.

By the time he announces that lunch is ready, I'm surprisingly famished.

'Do you swim in the river here during the summer?' I ask as we take our seats.

'I used to as a child. My mother would get our driver to bring us down here, and we'd spend the whole day, just the two of us.'

'Why did your parents never have any more children?' I quiz him. 'I would have thought once they had the heir, they'd be looking for a spare.'

'Last I heard, you have to be in the same room to procreate,' Sebastian answers drily. He paused as Anton came over with a bottle of rosé, pouring both of us a generous glass.

I take an appreciative sip before putting my glass firmly back on the table. 'I'd better go easy on the wine; I have another four-mile hike to do after this.' He just laughs at my petulant comment as a large bowl of Greek salad arrives, together with a basket of homemade pitta bread.

'You are a cold, hard man,' I grouch, helping myself to a large portion of salad before returning to our previous conversation. 'I wasn't aware that your mother and father were at loggerheads.'

Sebastian shrugs. 'They weren't, they just never saw each other. Once I went to university, my mother spent most of her time at the house in Mallorca. She only came home after he had his car accident, and then she settled in Dartmouth.'

'Didn't she like Blackmore? God, this pitta's divine.' I pull a second piece out of the basket.

'I just think it was always my father's ancestral pile. He was old school. Expected those below him to bow and scrape. And he had a bunch of hangers on – sycophants who hung on his every word while they spent his money. My mother hated all of them, and once I was no longer at home, she simply moved out. My father was more than happy to see the back of her as long as she didn't cause him any embarrassment.'

'I take it she wasn't quite as…' I pause, searching for a word that would describe his mother without giving too much offence.

'Eccentric,' he supplies with a chuckle.

'I was going to say *unconventional*.' He laughs out loud.

'Oh, she was always unconventional, and a great beauty in her day. My father was a very good catch, and I'm told that at first, he was smitten. But I think the very thing that attracted him to her began to grate very early on. Especially as she refused to play the doting duchess.'

'I'd love to see a photo of her in her heyday. She's pretty magnificent now – even when she's wearing odd shoes. She was actually wearing an honest to God tiara when she brought the photos to me.'

Sebastian grinned and took a sip of his wine. 'I can only assume it was proposal night.'

'You know about it?'

'Of course. It's been going on for years. My mother uses it as an excuse to get out her valuables.'

'Oh, poor Roger,' I lament sadly. 'He's waited for her all these years.'

Sebastian snorted. 'If she actually said yes, I think it would kill him. He loves the romance and drama of it all. At the end of the day, he's a solicitor in Dartmouth – he needs all the excitement he can get.'

I frown, picking up my own glass. 'So, you don't think he really wants to marry her?'

'Of course not. He wouldn't last five minutes. Trust me, they're both perfectly content with their relationship as it is.'

'I think they're very wise,' I muse. 'I dare say it keeps the juices flowing.'

'I'd rather not talk about juices and my mother in the same sentence if you don't mind,' Seb retorts with a shudder. 'Would you like any more salad?'

I shake my head, and ever attuned to our wants and needs, Anton steps up to take our plates away.

'Can I pour you some more wine, madam?' he asks when he returns.

I shake my head sorrowfully. 'I don't want to risk falling down a crevasse on the walk back.'

'This is south Devon, not the Alps,' Sebastian counters, holding out his own glass.

'Ok, just the one,' I relent. 'Do we have pudding?'

'Of course, Ms. Shackleford. I can offer you a selection of cheese and biscuits or our chef's special homemade chocolate brownie with clotted cream.' I narrow my eyes to make it look as though I'm actually deliberating, before giving a small scoff and saying, 'Is there even a contest?'

'I believe not, madam.' He turns to Sebastian. 'What can I bring you, your grace?'

'You have to ask?' Seb grins.

Anton inclines his head and goes off to fetch our puddings. 'Oh, and could you bring Coco her treat now,' Seb calls after him. I look down at Coco whose head has immediately lifted at the sound of her name.

'You know, I forgot she was there,' I comment, feeling guilty. 'She's very well trained. Nothing at all like Dotty. The greedy madam would have been up on the table by now.'

'Collies are generally very intelligent and quite easy to train,' he responds, smiling down at his dog who was well aware we were talking about her and wagging her tail hopefully.

'What about whatever she's crossed with?' I ask, reaching out to give her a quick fuss.

'If I knew what it was, I'd tell you,' he responds, just as Anton arrives back with our brownies. After depositing the plates on the table, he puts his hand into his pocket and pulls out... something. Coco clearly knows exactly what it is, and she does a little happy dance before sitting up beautifully, her entire body like a statue apart from her tail.

'It's a Yak bone,' Sebastian explains. 'Made from Yak milk I believe. Coco loves them.'

I laugh as she takes her prize right over the other side of the glade to eat. Obviously making doubly sure that nobody can take it off her.

'Have you decided what you're going to do about the photos?' Sebastian asks. I blink, for a second blindsided by the sudden change in conversation. By unspoken consent, we've both purposely kept the subject of my mother out of the day.

I shake my head and shrug. 'I'm not sure there's anything I can do aside from trying to find out who our mystery man is. The police won't be interested in a few grainy pictures of a happy family, not without good reason.'

'So, we need to find out who this mysterious possible member of the Imperial family is.'

I nod. 'But if she sent the photos to me for safekeeping, maybe she doesn't actually want me to do anything with them at all, except put them somewhere they can't be found.' I take a bite of my brownie, then lay down my spoon, my appetite suddenly lost. 'If she's been with him all these years, and he *does* have connections, there's got to be some record of it somewhere. When I get into the office tomorrow, I'll start digging, hopefully without alerting whoever it is she's scared of. If I find anything conclusive, I'll hand the whole lot over to Interpol. I'm not stupid, Seb.'

'I never said you were, sweetheart. What if whoever she's scared of discovers you have the photos and comes after you?'

I sigh and drain my glass. 'There's nothing to say they don't already know.' Suddenly cold, I tuck my arms inside my fleecy jacket. 'I'm so sorry I've dragged you into this. Do you want me to stay away until it's all over?'

'So, I do what? Hole up in Blackmore with my head up my arse until the danger's past? Surely you know me better than that, Teddy.'

I bite my lip, absurdly grateful that he's not prepared to simply abandon me to the circling wolves.

I glance up at the sky then down at my watch. 'Bloody hell, we'd better get going, it's past one thirty and we still have a two-hour hike to do.'

Seb leans back in his chair and grins at me. 'Jamie's bringing the car over. He'll be waiting for us at the end of the track at two.' As his words register, I feel a sudden surge of love for this amazing man who clearly thinks of everything.

'We still have twenty minutes. If you've finished, we'll leave Anton to clear up and walk along the river a little way before cutting up to the track.' I nod, my heart still too full to speak.

As we move, Anton rushes over to help me with my chair. 'Thank you, Anton, everything has been lovely,' I manage, my voice coming out ridiculously hoarse.

'You're very welcome, Ms. Shackleford,' he beams.

Seb calls Coco to us, and she immediately runs over and drops the remainder of her bone at his feet. 'Don't want to leave it, heh?' He bends down to ruffle her fur and without hesitation, picks up the now slobbery bone and tucks it into his pocket, wiping his hand on his sweatshirt. I cringe, then laugh.

'That's disgusting,' I chuckle. 'It'll have fluff all over it now as well as dribble and dirt.'

'She'll just think it adds to the flavour,' he grins taking my hand. Fortunately, it's the one that hasn't touched the yak bone.

We stroll along the river in companionable silence watching Coco as she dashes happily backwards and forwards along the trail. After about half a mile, we turn away from the river to follow another track back to civilisation. I feel a sudden pang at the thought, exacerbated when he says, 'What time do you want to head back to Dartmouth?'

'After dinner?' I respond. No sense in going back to toast and marmite until I have to.

He nods and smiles. 'I'll tell Jamie to bring the car round for us at eight.'

I frown, suddenly realising what he said. 'Us?' I query.

He looks over at me. 'Well, I know full well you won't come and stay over at Blackmore until this whole thing is finished, so, if you've no objections, Coco and I will come and stay with you instead.'

CHAPTER 9

'Right then, Mabel, your shift starts at ten. I'll give you a twenty-minute head start, then you can pop down and let me in.'

They were sitting at the table in the Admiralty kitchen. Mabel had just made him some poached eggs on toast. Charles Shackleford was firmly of the opinion that whoever thought up the idea of poaching a bloody egg should have been made to walk the plank. In his book, the only way to eat an egg was fried, preferably in bacon fat. But Mabel had this ongoing obsession with his arteries. And on this occasion, in the spirit of wanting to keep her sweet, he gave every indication of tucking into his egg with enthusiasm. Which is why her next words nearly had him reaching for the frying pan.

'I'm really not very sure about this, Charlie. The lady who interviewed me was so nice, and I'm just not comfortable letting you in under the covers.'

The Admiral put down his knife and fork with a baffled frown. 'What the bloody hell are you on about, Mabel. I've got no intention of indulging in a spot of hanky-panky in the bloke's bed.'

'Of course not,' she retorted, shocked. 'But I'm not happy with all this under the covers, creeping about. If I let you in to search that man's bedroom, I'll be breaking the law. I could end up in prison. I'll be a fallen woman.'

'I'm pretty sure you won't,' muttered Charles Shackleford under his breath. 'My angel,' he said out loud, 'there is no need for you to worry your pretty head. I'll be in and out like a ghost. No one will know I've been there. I'll even help you make the bed before I leave.'

His heart sank as Mabel pursed her lips. Bugger, she was about to dig her heels in.

'No, Charlie, I've made up my mind. I will be the one doing the searching. You'll just have to tell me what I'm looking for.'

The Admiral stared at her silently for a few seconds. All was not lost. It could work. 'We'll have to stay in full radio contact,' he insisted. Then he had a thought. 'We could use that *WhatsApp*, then I'd be able to see you.'

'What's that?' Mabel asked.

'No, *WhatsApp*,' the Admiral repeated. 'Have you got your hearing aids in?' He pulled his mobile phone out of his pocket. 'Victory put it on my phone when she was in France. Said I could call her for free. I think she put it on yours too.'

Mabel went to get her phone out of her handbag. 'It's that green square with the telephone in the middle,' he told her when she sat back down.

'I've never noticed that before,' she commented. 'What do I have to do?'

'I'm not sure, wait a minute, let me have a shufti.' Charles Shackleford touched the app to open it and immediately three names came up. Victory, Noah and Mabel. He pressed on Mabel's name and then had three choices – one of which was video. 'Right then, Mabel, get ready.'

He pressed the video picture and almost immediately he could see himself on the screen. He nearly dropped the phone. Bloody hell, there's close and there's too bollocking close. He could see his nose hairs.

Mabel's phone began to ring. 'Ooh, there's a tick and a cross,' she flapped, 'I'll press the tick.' A second later, he was relieved to see his face replaced by Mabel's.

'Oh, I say,' she enthused, 'I can see you really clearly, Charlie.'

'That's because I'm sitting three bloody feet away,' the Admiral retorted. 'The signal might not be so good in the *Seven Stars*. Still, whatever happens, we'll be ready for it, old girl. Nothing like a self-adjusting cock up to keep us on our toes. We'll call it *Operation Nick Nack.*'

THE SCARIEST PART of Sebastian's offer to come and stay with me was my instinctive reaction to it. In one word - happiness.

I was elated, over the moon, exhilarated, delighted… I could go on, but I think I'm painting the right picture. Naturally, it being me, hard on its heels came pure dread, not to mention panic. Had I left the place a mess? Did I have any food in that wasn't more than a week out of date? Would I have to *cook* for him? And lastly, what if we *hate* each other?

All the way back to Dartmouth my mind was playing increasingly awful scenarios, until we reached the outskirts of town, and I finally managed to halt the runaway train. Seb and I have stayed together for longer than a weekend before. We were in France for nearly three weeks, and we never argued once. In fact, it had been wonderful.

My first reaction when he asked to stay was the right one. Everything that came after was just that crappy voice in my head doing its thing.

And this morning? Well, this morning I admit to waking up full of the joys of spring. Which in all the movies is about the time disaster usually strikes.

Seeing Seb's head on the pillow next to mine and Coco curled up in her basket at the foot of the bed is more than just nice. It's *comfortable*. 'What would you like for breakfast?' I ask after he leans over to kiss me sleepily.

'You mean you've actually got something edible?' he teases.

'Depends on your definition of edible. I don't think the bread has any mould on it. Well, I couldn't see any last night, but in fairness it was quite dark.'

'A bit of mould is like taking penicillin,' he grins. 'What about Marmite?'

'Of course, I'm not a complete philistine.'

Half an hour later we're both showered and ready for the day. In my case, work.

'I just realised you haven't got a car here,' I frown, giving my last piece of toast to Coco. 'Do you need to be anywhere, or will you be okay on two legs?'

'If I need to go further than my own nose, I'll take my life in my hands and borrow my mother's,' he answers picking a bit of mould off the edge of his bread. I wince, promising to pick up a fresh loaf on my way home.

'Not a chance,' he counters. 'I'm fully conversant with your shopping methods. I'll take over the feeding of us while I'm here.'

The old me would have immediately bristled at such an autocratic announcement, but all the new me can think about is the possibility of a lasagne that doesn't come out of a box.

'I take it that look on your face means you'd like me to make pasta?' he laughs.

'Lasagne – and I'll love you forever,' I respond fervently, bending down to pull my boots on. I'm joking, but as I straighten back up, I catch an expression of such intensity on his face, that my heart jumps into my throat. A second later, he gives his customary lazy grin, and I wonder if I imagined it.

'First things first – I'd better go and inform my mother I'm slumming it in her garden...'

'I prefer the term glamping,' I interrupt with a chuckle. 'Gives a whole different connotation.'

'Glamping it is then. Anyway, once I've announced my presence, I'll take Coco out for a walk, then head into town to do some shopping. Can I leave her with you while I brave Marks and Spencer's?'

'Of course,' I answer climbing to my feet. 'Can you bring me and Alex lunch while you're at it?'

He lifts his eyebrows and regards me in a way that has me wondering if we've got time to go back to bed. Then he sighs dramatically, muttering, 'Just call me Cinders.'

Ten minutes later, I'm walking along the side of the river and my mind goes back to the curious expression on his face. It's not the first time I've spotted it. He had it on Saturday and again during the picnic yesterday. I don't *think* I'm imagining it. After all, I'm an ex-copper and used to picking up inadvertent cues in people's expressions. Is he getting tired of our relationship as I believed on Saturday?

Or could he actually be thinking of taking it to the next level?

I don't know which scares me the most...

* * *

'WHAT'S YOUR SIGNAL LIKE, MABEL?' They were both standing outside the *Seven Stars*. Mabel dutifully pulled out her phone.

'I've got two bars.'

'Should be enough. I'll be close by, so let me know as soon as you get into Nick Nack's room.'

'How will I know I'm in the right room?'

'It's a bit bloody late to ask that now,' the Admiral grumbled, though his anger was mostly at himself for not considering the problem earlier. 'I reckon it'll be the one with stuff in it that looks foreign.'

Mabel nodded, too nervous to question what exactly constituted *foreign stuff*. She took a deep breath, then stiffened her spine, remembering her vital role in *Operation Murderous Marriages* at Berry Pomeroy Castle. In fairness, *vital* might well be a little bit of an exaggeration since she couldn't recall exactly what she'd done, but she was reasonably sure it had been helpful.

'*WhatsApp* me as soon as you're in position,' the Admiral was saying, patting her on the back in a show of camaraderie.

Mabel nodded, resisting the urge to salute. *Operation Nick Nack* was on.

* * *

'So, you think the man in these photos was the guy your mother ran off with?' Alex frowns, looking down at the pictures. 'And he's the same man she mentions meeting when she first arrived in Japan – the one distantly connected to the Imperial family?'

'It makes sense when you think about it,' I respond. 'She practically vanished off the face of the earth as far as Dad and I were concerned. All these years I thought she'd gone off with Aki, but her total lack of communication...' I trail off and shrug. 'We just put it down to the *Yakuza* involvement.'

'Understandable given they ransacked your house and forced you out of Japan,' Alex declares.

'I think that may well have been part of it. But I also think any liaison between a member of the Imperial Family – however tenuous the link – and a gaijin would be hugely embarrassing, especially if it involved an illegitimate child.' I frown and shake my head, knowing I'm still missing something. 'If my mother has been a happily kept woman all these years, something drastic has to have happened to bring her out into the open.'

'It's a pretty big assumption to suppose she was happy,' Alex countered. 'Are you sure it's not what you *want* to believe?'

I give a derisory snort. 'I don't give a rat's arse about my mother's happiness or otherwise. She walked away from me and Dad without a backward glance.' I'm aware that my voice is shriller than usual. Alex looks at me with infuriating sympathy. I can tell he doesn't entirely believe my declaration of not giving a toss.

'These are just theories anyway,' I add briskly. 'But I can't just sit here twiddling my thumbs, waiting for my mother's next move. I'm not her bloody side kick. I need to find out what the hell is going on. And that means finding a concrete link.'

'I get it,' is all Alex says. 'And I'm on it.'

We spend the next hour in silence, and despite my frustration, I enjoy the sense of working with someone who knows how my mind works. Alex and I have always worked well together. If I'm being entirely honest, he was the reason I kept my job in the NCA as long as I did.

At just after ten, the bell rings. 'It's a bit early to be Sebastian,' I frown, climbing to my feet. 'He's going to leave Coco with us while he shops.' I ignore Alex's raised eyebrows as I go and answer the door. To my complete surprise, the Admiral is standing on the other side. And he's wearing an expression on his face that I've never seen before. After a second, I recognise it. Abject fear. My uncle is terrified.

'You've got to help me,' he blusters, crying openly. 'He's got Mabel.'

CHAPTER 10

$\mathcal{M}$abel had never done any actual chambermaiding before, but strangely enough found herself enjoying it. There was something satisfying about straightening someone's room, knowing they were on holiday. She didn't know why that should be, but was content to refresh their bathrooms, make their beds, and tidy their things.

In the first two rooms there was nothing to indicate that the person staying in the room was anything other than British, but the third one she entered – well, if she hadn't been told its occupant was Japanese, she might well have guessed because of the ornate pair of lacquered chopsticks that had been left on the dressing table. Her heart began to beat faster, and she sat down on the bed, rummaging around in the pockets of her apron for her mobile phone. Pulling it out, she searched for the green button Charlie had shown her and pressed it. But she had no idea what to do next. Sighing, she sent him a text instead. *I'm in the bedroom.*

Seconds later, her phone rang, and she was staring down into Charlie's face. 'Are you in position?' he whispered.

'Yes,' she whispered back.

'Right then, show me the room.'

'How do I do that?'

'Turn the bollocking phone around, Mabel.'

'Oh, right.' Obligingly, she turned the screen outwards and waved it around.

'Slow down a bit, you're making me feel bloody seasick.'

Climbing to her feet, Mabel held the phone in front of her and did a circuit of the room.

'Well, you won't need to do much tidying in there, old girl. If it weren't for the chopsticks and his toothbrush, you'd never guess the room was even occupied.'

'What am I looking for?' Mabel whispered urgently, her nerves getting the better of her.

'Anything with Agnes's name on it. Or Teddy's, for that matter. Search his drawers.'

'I am certainly *not* going through his underwear, Charlie. What do you think I am?'

There was silence for a second, then, 'Bollocking hell, Mabel, I mean the *chest* of drawers, not the bloke's underwear. Although you might need to poke 'em out of the way to look underneath. You could use his chopsticks.'

With a sigh, the matron placed the phone onto the top of the chest of drawers but decided to check the bedside cabinets first. A quick look through the one nearest her revealed a Gideon's Bible and a packet of jelly babies but nothing else. She hurried round to check the other cabinet. This time she had a little more luck, as the second drawer contained a notebook and pen.

Ignoring her beloved's heated whisper of 'What the hell are you doing, Mabel? All I can see is the bollocking ceiling. By the way, I think that light might need a bit of a dust,' she picked up the book and opened it. Unfortunately, the writing was all in Japanese – nothing at all in English. Disappointed, she placed it back in the drawer, taking care to leave it in exactly the same position. She was getting the hang of this spying lark.

'Are you there, Mabel?'

Next, she went over to the wardrobe. Inside were two white shirts, a black jacket, and two pairs of black jeans. In sudden inspiration, she rummaged through the jacket pockets and unearthed an empty packet of jelly babies and a Marks and Spencer's receipt. She looked at the slip with interest. He'd been buying sushi. She'd tried some of that up at Tory and Noah's but the raw fish had played havoc with her hernia.

'Have you found anything yet, Mabel?' The whisper from the top of the drawers was definitely getting more animated.

Closing the wardrobe door, she finally went back over to the chest of drawers. It was no good; she was going to have to rifle through the man's smalls. Sighing, she picked up the phone and propped it against the mirror, revealing the Admiral's face.

'Finally,' he muttered. 'Have you found anything?'

She shook her head, then frowned and leaned closer to the phone. 'I'm going to have to get the clippers on your nose hair Charlie.'

'Never mind my bloody nose hair. We're running out of time, Mabel. You must have found out *something* about him.'

'Well, I can tell you he likes jelly babies and sushi,' she answered. 'Oh and he wears a lot of black.' Then with a pained sigh, she picked up one of the chopsticks and pulled open the top drawer of the dresser.

Predictably, it contained several pairs of black boxer shorts.

The Admiral felt his frustration begin to boil over as he watched her gingerly poke the chopstick inside the drawers, pushing the pants this way and that, until suddenly his attention was drawn towards the door. The slowly *opening* door…

'I don't think there's anything else in here,' Mabel was saying.

'*Mabel*,' he hissed urgently, she looked up at him.

'You'll just have to wait, Charlie,' she muttered leaning further into the drawer. 'Rifling through a perfect stranger's underpants is more than any respectable woman should be expected to do. And I've only got one chopstick.'

The Admiral stared in speechless fear at the diminutive figure now standing in the open doorway. Incongruously, he found himself wondering if sushi was all the bloke ate. He'd seen more fat on a cold chip.

'*Mabel*,' he all but shouted.

'What,' she answered crossly, straightening. A pair of black underpants hung over the top of her chopstick.

'Behind you,' the Admiral whispered desperately.

Mabel's face went pale as she finally grasped his meaning. Swallowing, she turned and faced the stranger in the doorway.

'What do you think you are doing?' The small man's voice was cold and clipped as he strode into the room.

Heart in his mouth, the Admiral could only watch helplessly as Mabel waved the underpants on the end of the chopstick like a flag of surrender. Then she stepped back into the chest of drawers, causing it to bang against the wall. The room began to wobble on the screen as the phone slowly toppled sideways and fell onto the floor. Seconds later everything went dark.

I'VE NEVER SEEN my uncle in such a state. Waving him inside, I hold up my hand, halting his tirade. 'Slow down, Uncle Charlie. You need to tell me clearly and concisely what's happened.'

'I think the *Yakuza* have got Mabel,' he sobs. I throw a bewildered look over at Alex.

'Right, sit down and start at the beginning.' I push him unceremoniously into my chair and hold out a tissue.

Five minutes later, I want to strangle him. 'And you say this man's staying at the *Seven Stars*?' The Admiral blows his nose and nods.

'Which room is he staying in?'

'I don't know. I didn't ask Mabel the room number.'

'Why didn't you go into the pub?'

'I tried, but all the doors were locked. Short of climbing up the bollocking drainpipe, I couldn't get in.' Clearly, the Admiral we all know and love is beginning to resurface.

'I'm surprised you didn't try,' I mutter.

'I did try,' he announces at the same time, 'but the only window I could see open was the men's toilet and I'd need to have been bloody Houdini to squeeze through that – not to mention the fact that I'd have ended up headfirst in the urinal.' He shook his head sorrowfully. 'I'd have been no help to Mabel then.'

I swallow the urge to tell him he's not exactly been a bloody knight in shining armour up until now, but I bite my tongue, saying instead, 'Well, I doubt very much he'll have dragged Mabel kicking and screaming through the streets of Dartmouth.'

'What if he's... murdered her?' The Admiral whispers the last word, and I want to scoff, but inexplicably it sticks in my throat.

'Unlikely,' Alex declares. 'Whoever this man is, he's obviously keeping a low profile. Leaving a trail of dead bodies in his wake has a tendency to make people sit up and take notice.'

'I assume you've tried calling Mabel's phone?' I ask.

'Just goes to answerphone. I think it must have broken when it fell off the chest of drawers.'

I look over at Alex. 'Obviously, we need to get over to the *Seven Stars* – I'd appreciate your backup.'

He nods, immediately getting up from his chair, just as the doorbell rings again. 'Bloody Grand Central Station's got nothing on this place,' I grouch, pushing myself away from the desk. A second later, I throw open the door to see Mabel and an unknown Japanese man standing on the threshold.

* * *

'REALLY, darling you don't have to stay in a shed, there's plenty of room here.' Sebastian pushed down his irritation at his mother's comment.

'It's hardly a shed, mother, and you're perfectly content to allow Teddy to stay there.'

'Teddy is not the Duke of Blackmore,' she retorted. 'And neither, the last time I looked, was she the Duchess. Unless of course there's something you haven't told me.'

Sebastian narrowed his eyes. His mother was almost impossible to read. Her tone was mild, but that really didn't mean anything. Eccentric she might be, but he suspected that at least some of it was put on when she wanted to avoid doing something.

'No, Teddy and I didn't get married while you weren't looking, if that's what you're asking.'

His mother chuckled. 'She's a lovely girl and you could certainly do a lot worse. Apart from her mother of course. Perfectly dreadful woman as far as I can tell. I do hope she hasn't got any more skeletons in her cupboard. But then, what's left of the British aristocracy are mostly as mad as a sack of ferrets anyway. I blame the interbreeding.'

'Thank you, Mother,' Sebastian retorted drily.

'Oh, I don't mean you darling, you've got a long way to go before you turn into an imbecile. But you only have to look at me to know it's unavoidable. Perhaps you should mention it to dear Teddy before you pop the question.'

Sebastian gritted his teeth and gave a deliberately nonchalant shrug. 'I'm simply staying with her for a few days, that hardly constitutes a lifelong commitment.'

'Well, she'd be a fool to turn you down if you asked her, dotty genes or no,' his mother declared loyally. She paused for a second before adding, 'And I have to say I think she'd be a breath of fresh air in our pretentious, over precious circles. I for one will be demanding a ring-side seat when she's introduced to Royalty ...'

Ten minutes later, Sebastian managed to escape, and he took Coco up to Gallant's Bower. As they tramped through the woods, he reflected on his mother's words. Clearly in her customary scatterbrained manner, she was telling him she approved of Teddy. But her comment about royalty had made him wince a little.

And then of course there was the subject of children. After Carla, he had thought himself reconciled to the fact that the title would die with him. But since Teddy, no matter how much he tried to dismiss it, the possibility of an heir came back to haunt him.

And that was the whole crux of the matter.

It wasn't just whether Teddy would consider marrying him or not. If she flatly refused to make their relationship legal, he would still willingly live with her in unwedded bliss for the rest of their lives.

Except for children. If any son they had was born out of wedlock, he wouldn't be able to inherit the dukedom.

'THIS IS MATSUI YOSHIMATSU,' Mabel manages to say before she's suddenly dragged into my uncle's arms in true *Gone With The Wind* fashion. Both Alex and I are rooted to the spot in astonishment, while our new Oriental friend is forced to take a step backwards to avoid a sudden impromptu threesome.

As they finally part, Mabel becomingly pink, Alex and I manage to persuade the Admiral that decking her supposed kidnapper is in nobody's best interests and ten minutes later everyone is sitting down except Alex who's hurriedly making coffee.

'Mr Yoshimatsu,' I say carefully, 'please accept my apologies for my aunt and uncle's … err … imprudent decision to take the law into their own hands in searching your hotel room, but may I ask what reason you have for being in Dartmouth?'

'Before he tries to tell you otherwise, that wasn't his bollocking room either. He's not the same bloke I spoke to on Saturday.' The Admiral glares at the small man who, for a second, does nothing. Then, giving my uncle a wary look, he stands up and gives a small bow.

'As the good lady said, my name is Matsui Yoshimatsu. I am from the Japanese National Police Agency.

'I believe we have a mutual interest in the whereabouts of your mother.'

CHAPTER 11

'*D*o you have any form of identification on you?' I ask, my voice sharp. I am currently resisting the urge to throttle my idiot of an uncle.

He nods and puts his hand inside his jacket, seconds later handing me an ID card. I look down at it with a frown, then hand it back. 'This doesn't really tell me anything. Fake ID cards are easy to get.'

The small man nods in acknowledgement. 'You may telephone my superior. I work in the Organised Crime Division. I can give you his direct line if you wish.' He looked down at his watch. 'I believe the time in Tokyo will be about seven thirty p.m. He may still be in his office.' I shake my head.

'Alex, can you get hold of your contact in the NCA? Ask him to find out if the Japanese National Police Agency's Organised Crime Division have a Matsui Yoshimatsu on their books? Tell him it's urgent.'

Alex gives me a look but doesn't bother reminding me that his old colleagues in the NCA are likely up to their necks in it and will not take kindly to being asked for favours from someone who works for a local newspaper in the back of beyond. Instead, he hands out the coffees and informs me that he'll take the call in the back.

As he closes the door behind him, I turn back to Mr. Yoshimatsu. 'Perhaps you'd like to tell me why your NPA is interested in my mother?' I ask brusquely.

'I think perhaps you have your suspicions, Ms. Shackleford,' he responds softly. I stare at him, my heart slamming against my ribs.

'Do you know if my mother is safe?' I ask at length, pleased that my voice isn't wobbling – much.

'As far as we're aware, no harm has come to her. Yet. But we need to find her before … other interested parties do.'

'And was the bloke I met on Saturday one of these *other interested parties*?' the Admiral asks bluntly. 'Is Agnes in some kind of trouble? How do we know, you and old Nick Nack aren't in cahoots?'

Matsui spread his hands and gave a small shrug. 'I'm afraid I do not know any *Nick Nack* and the word *cahoots* is not familiar to me. However, I believe if my intentions were less than honourable, your fiancée would not be here.'

'So, you are nothing to do with the Japanese man my uncle spoke to on Saturday?' I favour said uncle with a frustrated glare which goes straight over his head.

'I bet he's Jacuzzi,' Mabel interrupts breathlessly. Matsui gives the matron a baffled look.

'You mean *Yakuza*,' I correct Mabel gently while fighting a sudden urge to laugh hysterically.

'What did this man say to you when you spoke to him in the public bar? I believe you called him *Nick Nack*? Is that an informal name commonly used here for a Japanese man?'

'No, it isn't,' I butt in hastily, giving my uncle another glare – which has the same effect as the first one.

'After that little chap in the James Bond film,' the Admiral explains airily. The detective simply stares at him, none the wiser.

'What did this man *actually* say to you?' I ask my uncle curtly as Alex walks back into the room.

Puffing himself up, the Admiral recounts the whole conversation. 'He wanted me to read him that article you wrote for the Herald, Teddy, so he's definitely interested in you. And he made it clear that Agnes wasn't a friend. In fairness, I doubt he's actually got any. His smile was enough to give any normal person bloody nightmares. He had that many gold teeth, he should be sleeping with his head in a safe.'

'I do not know his real name,' Matsui says thoughtfully, 'so with your permission, I will continue to refer to him as Nick Nack. And I believe you are correct; he is staying in the room you searched. I was about to do the same when I encountered your fiancée.'

'There was a notebook in the bedside cabinet,' Mabel adds excitedly.

I look at the detective. 'Did you take it?'

He shakes his head. 'I did not wish to alert our friend to my presence. But I was able to take photographs of the pages with writing on them. I have not yet had the opportunity to read them.'

'Perhaps now would be as good a time as any,' I suggest.

'If I share my findings with you…'

'Actually, the notebook was my finding,' Mabel interrupts firmly.

Matsui bends his head towards the matron, still determinedly polite. 'As you say.' Then he turns back to me and continues, 'Perhaps you will do me the same courtesy.'

'I will willingly share what I know once your identity has been confirmed, Mr. Yoshimatsu. As long as I believe you have my mother's best interests at heart.'

The small man stares at me for a second, his face inscrutable. 'I do not believe we have much time,' he declares at length. 'So, with your permission, I will return here tomorrow morning in the hope that we can …' he pauses, obviously searching for the right word.

'Collaborate?' I suggest helpfully.

He nods, then gives a deep bow. 'Until tomorrow.' Seconds later, he's gone.

As the door shuts behind him, I finally turn to my uncle, ready to tear a strip off him. However, just as I'm about to launch into one of my once infamous set downs, I catch the tender look he gives Mabel, and just like that, my anger fades. He'd been truly frightened for her. Hopefully, he'll remember that fear when he thinks about doing anything even more stupid in the future. Okay, I know it's a forlorn hope, but still…

Instead of lambasting him, I say quietly. 'You do know that if it had been *Nick Nack* who'd caught Mabel in his room, she could well have been seriously hurt.'

He gives me a sheepish nod, but underneath his remorse, the gleam is still there, and I realise I might as well ask him to stop breathing.

So, rather than order him to mind his own bloody business in future, I take - for me – a slightly gentler approach. 'If you uncover anything else, Uncle Charlie, *please* can you just come to me with it? Whatever you do, don't take matters into your own hands. You're just lucky that nobody's been hurt so far during your solo investigations.'

He looks suitably contrite and promises to keep me apprised of any further developments. 'Come along then, Mabel, old girl. Let's get you home. Pickles hasn't had his walk yet, and his legs'll be in plaits.'

I shake my head and sigh as they totter through the door, arm in arm. Butter wouldn't melt...

Then, as the door shuts behind them, I turn to Alex. 'Do you think Matsui Yoshimatsu is the real deal?'

He gives a small shrug. 'We'll know soon enough. He's definitely lying about wanting to find your mother. I think he knows exactly where she is. I think the person he's come here to find is you.'

I stare silently at him for a second. 'You think he's after the photographs?'

'I think it's very likely that both of them are. The Admiral said this Nick Nack guy was interested in your article, which strangely enough, is entirely about you.' He pauses, and his mobile phone rings into the quiet. As he takes the call, I stare into space feeling a sudden disquiet.

Two men, both purportedly from Japan turn up in Dartmouth at the same time as my mother sends me an envelope full of photographs. It can't be coincidence.

'Matsui's legit,' Alex confirms as he cuts the call. 'Naturally, my contact wants to know what the bloody hell someone from the Japanese NPA is doing in Dartmouth. What do I tell him?'

I purse my lips thoughtfully. 'Nothing, yet, but we might need their help.'

'You think?' he retorts with a humourless chuckle. 'You might be slightly missing the point here, Teddy. If you are the person both men have come to find. You could well be at risk.' He holds his hand up to halt my interruption. 'So, we think one of them is a good guy, but the other? If he really is *Yakuza*, I doubt he'll be above using torture to get what he wants.'

'That's why Sebastian has come to stay,' I respond quietly. 'Obviously, he doesn't know yet that things are a little worse than we thought.'

'I take it you're going to tell him?'

'Of course. But I'm not sure you should tell Freddy.'

Alex grimaces, then shakes his head. 'I can't keep something like this from him. He'll never forgive me. But I will issue a gagging order.'

I look at him doubtfully. 'Tory knows about the photos as well. I showed them to her on Friday night.'

'Bloody hell, she's almost as nosy as Freddy. I think we might have to get them all round a table.'

I give a weary nod just as the doorbell rings. 'I really hope it's Seb this time,' I mutter, getting to my feet. Sure enough, as I open the door, a black and white bundle of fur dashes past me. And then, of course, I have to choose that moment to have a major wobble over the events of the last hour and I surprise Sebastian by throwing my arms around his neck as he steps into the room.

'Why don't I get a greeting like this every time?' he quips, stepping back and looking at me quizzically as he says hi to Alex.

'We've had an interesting morning.' Damn it, even my bloody voice is wobbling.

He immediately turns serious. 'What's happened?'

'I'll make another coffee while you fill him in.' I smile at Alex gratefully. Coco, of course, follows the biscuit trail.

Seb doesn't interrupt while I describe the events of the morning, and when I've finished, he sits thoughtfully for a second. That's another thing I love about him. The way his mind plays over a conversation before venturing a comment.

'Well, it certainly doesn't look as though we have the luxury to just sit tight on the photos and hope your mother turns up to play happy families.' He nods his thanks as Alex hands him a coffee. 'Your detective mentioned that he didn't think there was much time. Do you think he was simply trying to force your hand, or is he concerned that more goons are likely to come out of the woodwork?'

'He told us that he didn't know where my mother was, and implied that her life was in danger, but Alex thinks he's lying about not knowing her whereabouts. He gave no indication that he thinks Nick Nack has a few friends on the way.' I spread my hands and give a shrug. 'If I had to guess, I think it's more likely he's trying to force my hand.'

Seb looks over at Alex. 'You think Yoshimatsu knows about the photos?'

Alex nods. 'I think they both do. I think that's what they're here for.'

'I assume you told Alex your theory about your mother's illicit liaison?' Seb asks me as he sips his coffee.

I nod. 'We were looking for some kind of concrete connection when the Admiral turned up. But we thought we had more time.'

'So, the long and the short of it is that between now and when your detective turns up tomorrow morning, we need to find out what's so important about the damn photos.'

'Basically, yes,' I affirm.

'I'll work on it tonight,' Alex declares.

'You're going to tell Freddy everything?' I ask doubtfully.

'He has a unique way of looking at things,' Alex responds wryly. 'I actually think it could be useful.'

'Why don't you both come over to ours this evening?' Seb suggests. 'I'm making lasagne, and four heads are better than two.'

Despite the ridiculous thrill at hearing him refer to the Boathouse as *ours*, I actually think it's a good idea, if only to keep an eye on Freddy.

'It'll be pretty cosy, but there's enough room for laptops and pasta,' I add.

'Good idea,' Alex grins. 'Then we'll all be able to keep an eye on Freddy ...'

Alex and I spend the rest of the afternoon trawling the internet for any mention of my mother after she retired from the ring, but there's nothing. Every scrap of information about her, apart from the recent lurid newspaper headlines and subsequent interview, is from the very start of her wrestling career in Japan. And then it's retrospective – the internet back then really wasn't quite the mine of information that it is now. There's nothing at all to indicate what she's actually been doing during the intervening years.

And going through her recent interview again, I'm struck by how vague it actually is. Aside from her account of meeting a distant relative of Japanese royalty when she first arrived in Japan, she talks about her love for sumo wrestling, her regret at leaving me – there was no mention of any sadness at abandoning my dad – and all her humorous anecdotes could actually be referring to anybody.

Frowning, I sit back in my chair. My conviction that she was trying to tell me something grows, but unfortunately, I think she might have imbued me with more intelligence than I actually possess because right at this moment I still can't fathom what it is ...

CHAPTER 12

'God, that smells amazing,' I breathe as I walk through the door. 'Can I keep you?'

He looks over at me and grins, while Coco throws herself into my arms in excitement. Clearly, the two hours she's been away from me have been far too long. Laughing I carry her to the sofa and sit down next to my handsome chef.

'Of course, you could have cooked the whole thing with just a frilly apron on,' I say, leaning over to give him a kiss.

'Trust me, the risks far outweigh the benefits,' he pronounces, putting his arm around my shoulders and pulling me to him to kiss me properly. 'Fancy some garlic bread?' he asks when we finally break apart several minutes later.

'I've died and gone to Heaven.'

He climbs to his feet with a wink and goes over to the oven. 'How's your afternoon gone,' he asks, pulling out the deliciously pungent French stick.

'I think my mother has an unrealistic opinion of my intelligence,' I sigh, kicking off my boots. 'Which is not entirely surprising since she doesn't know me at all.'

I watch greedily as he places the basket of bread on the coffee table.

'Not for you, sweetie,' I tell Coco, 'it will make you poorly.'

'She's just had her dinner, so believe me, she's not hungry,' Seb counters, handing me a plate.

'What's that got to do with it? I would still eat this if I was bursting at the seams. It's not the only garlic stick you've made, is it?' I take a bite and close my eyes in ecstasy. 'If it is, Freddy and Alex will just have to go without.'

'I have another one ready to go.' He hands me a glass of wine. 'Did you find anything on the internet about your mother and our mystery man?'

'Nothing,' I mumble with my mouth full.

'I found something interesting,' he comments, helping himself to a piece of bread before sitting back down on the sofa.

I look over at him, eyebrows raised.

'I started researching the Japanese Imperial family. Japan's history is fascinating, but my interest has always been in the distant past - I know very little about its more recent history other than who the Emperor is and who's currently his successor. But I had no idea that, after the second world war, the size of the Imperial family was drastically reduced from twelve branches to one.' He pauses to take a bite out of his garlic bread, and I wait impatiently while he chews.

'Did the Emperor decide the hangers on had to go?' I ask.

He shakes his head. 'I don't think it was quite like that. It was more to do the with policies of the occupying forces after the war was over. Possibly because they vastly reduced the amount of money given to the family by the state and were also looking to reduce the Emperor's influence.

'Anyway, all those booted out were relegated to commoners, which must have been a bit of a comedown. In fact, from the articles I read, some of them suffered serious hardship.'

'Were they cut off completely?' I query, taking a sip of my wine.

'I'm not entirely sure, but I did discover that of the eleven houses forced to leave, only six of them remain. I think they're now treated like distant poor relatives and invited round to the palace for tea occasionally. I've written the names of the remaining houses down, though you might have better luck pronouncing them than me.' He hands me a sheet of paper, and I read through the names.

'It's all very interesting, but I don't recognise any of them,' I comment at length, laying the sheet back on the table and helping myself to the last piece of bread.

'I didn't really expect you to,' he responds, 'but here's where it gets even more interesting. Japanese succession laws are quite convoluted, not to mention archaic. Basically, only male members can sit on the Chrysanthemum throne, and they must be descended from the patriarchal line. Removing so many members of the Imperial family meant that the pool of candidates for the job has been vastly reduced, ultimately leading to a very real succession crisis, because in the last forty years, only one male child has been born.'

'Blimey, it must be something in the water,' I quip. 'Still, I assume they have daughters. Why don't they just pass a law saying that the throne can pass to a woman?'

'That's one of the proposed methods of solving the crisis, but the old guard is resisting the very idea. Currently, when a female member of the Imperial family marries, she loses her royal status completely - she becomes a commoner and is forced to leave.'

I give a rude snort. 'You're right, it *is* bloody archaic. I'm guessing that you think my mother's mystery lover is a member of the now defunct royal line, which is why he said his grandfather was once part of the Imperial family.'

He grins at me. 'Bingo!'

'Well done, Sherlock.' I lean over to kiss him. 'Do you think my mother could have sent the photos because the relationship has gone sour? Could she be involved in some kind of custody battle?' I frown, holding out my now empty glass for a top up before adding, 'I can't imagine the Japanese organised crime division would be interested in a domestic, and it doesn't tell us why her life is suddenly at risk. No connection to the *Yakuza* either.'

'I still have no idea where they fit it,' Seb admits, doing his sommelier bit, 'but I think there's one possible reason her lover might want her out of the picture.' I look at him enquiringly and wait.

'As I said earlier, one of the ways the Japanese government is looking to solve the succession crisis is by allowing female members of the family to inherit the throne. But there are two others.

'Firstly, there are suggestions that the six remaining families of those kicked out in 1947 be simply given back their royal status. The second idea is... and I quote from Quora, "to reinstate former Imperial Princes or their male-line descendants as adopted children of current members of the Imperial family."'

'If the government goes with either of the second two choices, that will mean our mystery man could be up for a bit of a promotion.'

* * *

'I THINK you were very lucky it wasn't Nick Nack in that bedroom, Sir. Who knows what might have happened to Mabel?'

They were sitting on their customary stools at the bar in the *Ship*, and while they didn't usually do early doors on a Monday, the Admiral thought it wise to apprise Jimmy of the latest in *Operation Nick Nack*, though he had to say he was a bit disappointed in Jimmy's lack of enthusiasm – though that could have been because the small man wasn't actually aware there *was* an *Operation Nick Nack*.

'It was a bit of a bloody cake and arse party,' Jimmy lad, 'I'll give you that. But Mabel kept her head, and in the end, it all turned out all right.' He gave a small chuckle. 'A classic self-adjusting cock up.'

'Does this mean you'll do as Teddy asks?' Jimmy went on, much to the Admiral's discomfort.

'Well, I think Mabel's chambermaiding days are over,' he hedged. 'I'm going over there tomorrow to hand in her notice for her. I told her she's got to put her feet up after the shock she had today.'

'So, you're not intending to have another look at that man's room then?' Jimmy looked at his former superior narrowly.

'I don't think there was anything in it apart from the notebook, and that was all in bollocking Japanese.'

'So, you're just going to hand in Mabel's notice and nothing else?'

'Of course,' the Admiral blustered. 'What the bloody hell did you think I was going to do?' He sniffed and took a large sip of his pint.

This meeting wasn't going the way he'd planned at all. He'd been fully intending to tell Jimmy about *Operation Nick Nack*, but ever since they'd sat down, his friend had been acting like a bloody poodle faker. There was no way he'd agree to a spot of tracking. Still, he had to try.

'Why don't you come over with me?' he suggested casually. 'We could have a spot of breakfast in Alf's if you fancy.' He looked over at the small man with feigned nonchalance.

'That would be nice,' Jimmy responded, much to the Admiral's delight. 'Emily's off to Torquay for the day, so I'm at a bit of a loose end.'

Better and better. Charles Shackleford resisted the temptation to rub his hands together as Jimmy finished his pint. 'I'll be getting off now then, Sir,' he added, climbing down from his stool. 'What time do you want to meet?'

'Shall we say Alf's at around eight thirty?'

Jimmy frowned. 'That seems a little early, Sir.'

'Well, naturally I want to give them as much of a heads up as possible that Mabel won't be in,' the Admiral responded hastily. Truthfully, he was more interested in making sure he was in the vicinity when Nick Nack left the pub. Nevertheless, Jimmy nodded and gave a quick salute before heading out of the door.

The Admiral finished his own pint, then looked down at Pickles snoozing at his feet. 'Come on then, boy, time for dinner. Let's hope it's not them Italian tea-bags.'

As he walked back to his car, the Admiral fought the urge to do a little hop and a skip. He rummaged in his pocket to check he'd still got the tissue he'd half inched on Saturday, finally pulling it out in triumph. *Operation Nick Nack* was back on.

He was reasonably certain he'd find an opportunity during breakfast to tell Jimmy the plan. That was assuming he'd come up with one by then, of course…

* * *

'That was delicious, your grace and the pornographic images on the table were a nice touch. They definitely lent a certain piquancy to the pasta.'

'I'm pretty certain some of them are medically impossible,' I comment.

'You've clearly led a very sheltered life,' Freddy scoffs.

Sebastian grins. 'My mother's idea of a romantic weekend retreat is a little avant-garde, I'm afraid.'

'I'm really going to have to buy a tablecloth,' I sigh, standing up to collect the plates.

'Don't you dare,' Freddy retorts. 'They're a perfect ice breaker – especially when the conversation's a bit hard going.'

'Mum covered the table with a beach towel when they stopped here.' Alex laughs. 'She fell out with Dad when she kept catching him looking underneath.'

I return to the table with some chocolate. 'Coffee's on,' I tell them, 'so time to get down to business.' Plonking the chocolates in the middle of the table, I turn to Freddy. 'I assume Alex has brought you up to speed?' At his nod, I add, 'Seb did a bit of digging into the Japanese Imperial family, and he found something very interesting, but I'll leave him to tell you about it.'

While Sebastian brings them both up to date, I go and finish the coffee. By the time I get back to the table, he's finished giving them a convoluted account of his findings.

'Well, I suppose it gives him motive for wanting your mother out of his life,' Alex is saying.

'But what about his son?' I demand, sitting down. 'With the whole *boys are the best* policy that seems pretty entrenched in Japanese royal circles, he might not want to throw the baby out with the bathwater, so to speak.'

'So, let me get this straight,' Freddy declares. 'If our man is descended from the patriarchal line, it could mean he has a real shot at being one of the lucky adoptees, if that's the way they decide to go. But even if they just decide to bring all of the defunct families back into the fold, it would still give him a bloody good step up in Japanese high society.'

'And having a son already would give him a distinct advantage,' I add. 'But possibly not with a non-Japanese mistress in tow who also happens to be the boy's mother.'

'But we still need to know where the *Yakuza* fit into all this,' Alex counters. 'And given that they ransacked your house thirty years ago, they've had a connection to our prince-in-waiting for a bloody long time.' He pauses, clearly gathering his thoughts. 'So, I did some digging this afternoon, and an *I'll scratch your back if you scratch mine* relationship is not as preposterous as it initially sounds.

'Google wasn't really a thing back when Agnes first left, so there's very little specific information to be found, but there are various accounts of politicians with *Yakuza* connections in their families - I can name at least two who had *Yakuza* grandfathers. So, it's perfectly feasible that our man might have long had ties to a specific *Yakuza* family.'

'But why would they have ransacked our house?'

'If she was about to become the kept woman of someone important, perhaps they were looking to get rid of anything incriminating she might have left behind. They would certainly have wanted you and your father out of Japan.'

'And now, all these years later, with the possibility of gaining royal status, her lover could be cleaning house.' Sebastian's conjecture chills me to the core.

'So, he wants the son but not the mother basically,' Freddy clarifies, 'and he thinks the best way to do that is to bury her under someone's convenient patio and erase her entirely from his history.'

'But naturally he doesn't want to get his potentially royal fingers dirty, so he's getting his *Yakuza* friends to do it for him,' Alex picks up.

'But my mother is nothing if not canny,' I add, 'so she gets wind of his plan and goes into hiding, just as the story about me and Seb breaks. She contacts the newspaper and offers them an interview – mostly to let me know she's still alive. Then she sends me the photos as insurance.'

'But clearly her ex-lover knows you have them because his mafia buddies have sent someone to Dartmouth to retrieve them,' Sebastian finishes. Then he frowns, adding, 'We don't know how he found out though. It could be he's followed the same trail of breadcrumbs, or, as much as I hate to say it, it could mean he's discovered the where-abouts of your mother and is holding her against her will.'

'Matsui said this morning that he believes she's safe, and Alex thinks the detective knows where she is. If that's true, then it might mean the Japanese police have her in some kind of safe house. But if they're interested enough in this case to send someone from their organised crime division across to the other side of the world, it wouldn't be too bigger of a jump to assume our prince is more deeply embedded in the world of the *Yakuza* than simply a *you scratch my back* kind of way.'

'But we still don't know who the bastard actually *is*,' Freddy grumbles.

CHAPTER 13

*T*he rest of the evening we spent studying the Imperial House of Japan. There was plenty of information on the current house, but once we started looking into those who'd lost their status back in 1947, it got a lot more convoluted. There seemed to be thousands of them - okay that's probably a bit of an exaggeration, but to those of us whose Japanese is... well, *Japanese*, it just appeared as though the same names kept cropping up again and again, making the different members very difficult to distinguish.

There were very few pictures and none at all of anyone looking remotely like the man in my mother's photos. At just after ten, around about the time Alex accused Freddy of eating all the chocolates, we finally called it a day. I really didn't want to be responsible for the first post-marital spat between the newlyweds.

So, this morning I've woken with breath that would likely fell a grizzly at a hundred paces and a sense of doom akin to the onset of Armageddon. Fortunately, as well as Alex, Sebastian is going to be in the office when our friendly neighbourhood Japanese detective arrives. So that will be three of us putting him on the rack. That's if the poor chap doesn't keel over as soon as he walks through the door of course.

I'm eternally grateful that Freddy will be tied up with Hansel and Gretel all day…

* * *

THE ADMIRAL WAS UP and out of the door before Mabel had climbed out of bed. Moreover, he made doubly sure she'd remain there until he'd left by actually taking her a cup of tea. The fact that she'd narrowed her eyes and looked at him as though he was a cross between Casanova and Jack the bloody Ripper was a little perturbing, but Charles Shackleford told himself it was always good to keep a woman on her toes …

Though he wasn't meeting Jimmy until half-past eight, he was on the ferry by quarter to, since he needed to let Pickles get his morning ablutions out of the way, if the spaniel was going to do any tracking at all. Previous experience had taught him that getting Pickles to follow a scent before he'd done his morning business was like getting Tory to mind her own bloody business.

While he was following the spaniel around the park, poo bag at the ready, the Admiral found himself wondering whether he should be badgering Mabel a bit about setting a date for their nuptials. Now she had the *rock*, she seemed in no particular hurry to actually make it official. They'd been engaged for over a year now, but neither of them had broached the subject of a wedding. And lately, he'd found himself thinking a lot about Celia. The time he'd spent with Tory's mother felt like another life - so much so that sometimes it was almost as if it had happened to someone else. His relationship with Mabel was entirely different. It was comfortable – like a pair of worn in slippers. There was none of the fire and passion that had accompanied his first marriage – which was just as well, really. Any bedroom gymnastics would likely put him in traction.

Part of him wondered if they really needed to get married at all. But then he thought about Mabel's unexpected comments the day before. He suddenly realised he'd always seen himself as Mabel's rescuer – the man who'd liberated her from a life of drudgery.

But her words yesterday had made him sit up a bit. She was a bit of a dark horse was his Mabel, and it could well be that he was being a bit too bloody complacent. Maybe it was time to sweep her off her feet. As soon as *Operation Nick Nack* was over, he'd come up with a plan. Perhaps they could tie the knot somewhere a bit exotic, like Bournemouth. He'd have a word with Tory.

He was just debating on the possible merits of doing the whole thing at *Butlins* when Pickles finally decided to perform. It was perfect timing, giving him plenty of time to get to Alf's for half-past eight. Putting the spaniel back on his lead, Charles Shackleford strolled along the embankment, enjoying the early morning peace.

He was just approaching the Lower Ferry when, suddenly, out of the blue, he spotted Nick Nack hurrying down Lower Street in front of him. Blinking, thinking he was hallucinating for a second, the Admiral watched the man disappear round the corner, towards the ferry slip. Could he be intending to go across to Kingswear?

If so, what the bloody hell was he doing just standing here like a fart in a trance? Shaking his head, Charles Shackleford roused himself and hastened in the same direction, but as he turned the corner, and looked down the slip, there was no sign of the bloke. Well, he couldn't just have bollocking vanished. Grinding his teeth in frustration, the Admiral looked towards Bayards Cove twenty yards away. There was no sign of him. Bugger.

Berating himself for his slowness, Charles Shackleford looked down at Pickles who was sitting on the cobbles unconcernedly scratching behind his left ear. 'Right then lad, time for you to do your bit.' Pulling out the screwed-up tissue, the Admiral shoved it in front of the spaniel's nose, with the command, 'Find.' For a second, Pickles sniffed the tissue but didn't move. Then, abruptly, he stood up and put his nose to the ground. Seconds later, he was dragging the Admiral across the road to the fourteenth century Bayards Cove Inn not ten yards away. Once there, he sat down and wagged his tail. 'Bloody hell, Pickles, do you ever think about anything other than your stomach? It's not time for breakfast yet. *Find.*' The spaniel got to his feet but didn't move.

The Admiral sighed, really thinking his quarry had done a Houdini, but after Pickles gave a soft woof and yanked him towards the Inn door, Charles Shackleford finally peered through the windows. Moments later, he spotted Nick Nack sitting at a table near the back. And he wasn't alone. Trembling with excitement, the Admiral pulled out his mobile phone to call Jimmy.

The small man answered after the third ring. 'There's been a change of plan,' Charles Shackleford hissed. 'I'm in the Bayards. Get your arse in gear.' Then he cut the call, and stepped into the porch, edging round the newly erected Christmas tree. Bloody hell, they'd be putting the Christmas decorations up at Easter at this rate. With a sigh for the good old days, he pulled down his cap and pushed open the door.

DESPITE MY ANXIETY, I enjoy the walk along the Dart towards the town. Walking hand in hand with anyone is still a bit of a novelty to me, but I'm slowly losing the urge to snatch my hand away the moment Sebastian tries to take hold of it. As we walk, Coco trots along beside us, her nose in the air, enjoying the early morning briny smells emanating from the river below. For some strange reason, her inexplicable devotion to me shows no sign of waning, and she's settled amazingly well in my little chalet – which, given that it must be a bit of a comedown for her, pleases me a ridiculous amount.

'What time do you think our detective will arrive?' Seb asks. 'Have I got time to grab pastries?'

'I don't think the Japanese code of politeness will allow him to arrive before nine,' I respond, looking down at my watch.

'So, time for a strategy meeting then,' he retorts, 'and everyone knows proper strategizing is impossible without something sugary that's just come out of the oven.' He squeezes my hand and smiles down at me. I know he's deliberately keeping the tone light, and I'm absurdly grateful. Between Sebastian and Coco, I feel cocooned in a warm triangle, and for once I'm not fighting to free myself.

Coco and I go straight to the office, while Seb fetches the vital sugar rush. Alex is already there having apparently left early to avoid Freddy's early morning panto practice. 'There are only so many times I can listen to, *Stick out your finger so I can see if you're fat enough to cook*, without wanting to dig out the pliers,' he grouses.

Naturally, we'd both been pre-warned about Freddy's penchant for getting into character – even when half the cast are under eight. And while Tory's advice to remove all sharp objects until the panto is over had seemed a little excessive, the office is now without three pairs of scissors and a stapler…

'Do you think Yoshimatsu knows the identity of our former prince?' he asks as I set about making coffee.

'Almost certainly. Whether he'll deign to share the information with us…' I trail off with a shrug.

'Are you going to show him the photos?'

'I think I have to. As far as I can see, he's the only one who can protect my mother if her ex-lover's intent on burying her in someone's back garden.'

Alex gives a sigh as I put his coffee down in front of him. 'I don't know, it just seems a bit excessive. Why not simply pay her off?'

'Dead women can't tell any tales I suppose.'

'Is illegitimacy such a stigma in Japan?'

'I think it's not just the fact that my apparent half-brother was born out of wedlock. He was also born to a foreigner. With the huge importance the country places on the whole primogenitor thing, for a man who's potentially hoping to capitalise on his royal blood, it might well be catastrophic.' Alex nods just as the doorbell rings.

'I couldn't decide which ones,' Seb declares after I let him in, 'so I got a couple of everything.' He plonks the box onto the desk. The smell alone is almost orgasmic and for the next ten seconds, we engage in an undignified scrum. I'm hoping that the delightful cinnamon smell might help to drown out the collective smell of stale garlic that is undoubtedly permeating the air even now, and I tell myself that my second almond croissant is simply helping to foster English and Japanese relations. For the next couple of hours anyway …

'We're not expecting Daphne this morning, are we?' I ask, abruptly unable to banish the sudden horrifying picture of Mr. Yoshimatsu being questioned by our would-be newspaper mogul.

Seb shakes his head. 'She has bridge club on a Tuesday.'

I raise my eyebrows. 'I didn't realise quite how knowledgeable you are about your mother's day-to-day activities.'

'Do you blame me?' he counters drily. 'At the end of the day, I see my role as a kind of unofficial policeman whose job is to make sure she doesn't end up in jail or slapped with a lawsuit.'

'Not very likely at bridge club.'

'You'd be surprised. Haven't you read *The Thursday Murder Club*?'

'I thought keeping her out of trouble was our job,' Alex interrupts.

'I think of it as a three-pronged attack,' Seb responds. 'That way we cover all bases.'

'Why have you and I never had this discussion before?' I quiz him, narrowing my eyes.

'I didn't want you to dump me once you realised I was only dating you to keep an eye on my mother,' he deadpans.

'I think that might be a bit of a poisoned chalice, your grace,' I scoff. 'Have you forgotten I come with an uncle who fancies himself as Dartmouth's answer to Sherlock Holmes?'

'I agree he should come with a government health warning, but he did save me from a psychotic ex-wife.'

'God knows what would happen if they ever teamed up together,' Alex grins. 'I can see it now, *Mrs Sinclair and The Admiral*.'

'Or *The Admiral and the Dowager Duchess*,' I supply. 'Blimey I feel a book coming on. Move over *Richard Osman*.'

'I'll sue,' Sebastian retorts. 'Unless it's a best seller, of course.'

'Well, if you're looking for something in the *Stranger than Fiction* category, I might be better going for *The Sumo Wrestler and the Deadly Japanese Prince*,' I quip, dragging us back to the matter at hand.

'Can't see it catching on,' Sebastian counters with a mock frown. 'Everyone will tell you it's best to write in a series. No good writing a story that gets solved in one book.'

I flash him a grateful smile and follow it with a sigh before saying seriously, 'I think I'm going to have to share the photos with Mr. Yoshimatsu.'

Both men give a nod of agreement, just as the doorbell rings. 'But first we wait to see what he has to give us,' I add, climbing to my feet. 'And under no circumstances do we part with the originals.'

* * *

INTENT ON SLIPPING UNOBTRUSIVELY into the Inn just like that fellow used to do in the Milk Tray advert, the Admiral kept his eyes trained firmly on Nick Nack and slowly eased himself through the door - the very epitome of stealth. Unfortunately, he failed to notice that Pickles hadn't quite finished baptising the brand-new Christmas tree taking up half the front porch, and as the lead pulled taught, the spaniel found himself dragged up the tree which slowly began to topple towards the Admiral who was too busy being furtive to notice until the Christmas Angel knocked his cap off.

For a second, Charles Shackleford was convinced his cover had been blown, but fortuitously he managed to remain incognito throughout the whole fiasco owing to the fact that he had a large springer spaniel covered in bright red tinsel sitting on his head the very moment Nick Nack turned round to see what the commotion was.

Also fortunately, there were four members of staff on hand to pick both the tree and the Admiral up off the floor - though by this time, Pickles was shivering in the corner.

Still, his cover hadn't been blown - that was the main thing, and a couple of sausages would soon bring Pickles round. The main problem was that the staff were hanging around him like a bad smell, obviously concerned he was about to tell the world he'd been attacked by a rampaging Christmas tree. This generation were too soft. He thought back to the HMS Hermes incident in Thailand. If that had happened to some of the buggers who'd just joined, they'd be writing to their MP and going for bloody counselling.

Sighing, the Admiral sipped his coffee, making sure to keep an eye on Nick Nack. The bloke he was chatting with was facing the other way, so Charles Shackleford had no idea what the fellow looked like. Just that he had salt and pepper hair making him look older than his companion.

After about twenty minutes, a flustered Jimmy finally appeared at the door. Seeing him, the Admiral put his finger over his lips and gestured urgently. Frowning, Jimmy pushed open the door and hurried to the table. Once there, he hovered, looking at his former superior oddly.

'Sit down, Jimmy. You look like a lost fart in a haunted milk bottle.'

'Did you know you have tinsel in your hair, Sir?' Jimmy commented as he did as he was told.

'Remember we're under cover, Jimmy,' the Admiral hissed.

'I thought we were just having breakfast,' the small man responded, bewildered.

'We are, but we're having it under cover.'

'But why are we under cover, Sir?' Jimmy persisted, much to the Admiral's annoyance. 'They all know who we are in here?'

The Admiral gave a pained sigh. 'Nick Nack doesn't know who we are. And he's over there.'

Naturally, Jimmy immediately turned round to have a look, just as Charles Shackleford said, 'Don't look now.'

'I can't see him,' the small man answered.

The Admiral sighed in frustration. 'Take my word for it. He's in the corner at the back with some other chap.'

'Who's the other chap?' Jimmy asked.

'If I knew that, I wouldn't be calling him some other chap, would I? Bloody hell, Jimmy, sometimes I wonder how you got to Master at Arms with the instincts of a pot plant.'

'Is that why we're having breakfast here instead of Alf's?' Jimmy grumbled. 'I thought you said you weren't going to do anything else stupid or dangerous, Sir.'

'I never said anything of the sort,' the Admiral retorted. 'And anyway, all we're doing is keeping an eye on a dodgy Japanese bloke.'

With his heart sinking faster than you could say *spring roll*, Jimmy was inordinately relieved when they were interrupted by the waiter. 'Morning, Admiral, Jimmy,' he said cheerfully. 'What can I get you?'

'We'll have two large English breakfasts and a pot of tea, please,' Charles Shackleford returned promptly. Sighing, Jimmy closed up his menu and gave a weak smile up at the waiter. The sympathy in the man's eyes definitely made him feel a little better.

'Hang on, Jimmy lad, I think his mate's getting up from the table. No, no he isn't, he's sat back down again.' He looked over at the small man in frustration. 'Do you reckon you could get close enough to earwig?' he demanded.

'Why can't you do the earwigging?' Jimmy retorted.

'Because he knows what I look like. Come on, Jimmy, get a bloody grip.' He leaned forward to speak in a conspiratorial whisper that would undoubtedly have been heard by everybody on the surrounding three tables had there been anyone on them.

'Just pretend you're looking for brown sauce. People always want brown sauce.' He gave an encouraging nod and at length, Jimmy pushed back his chair with a sigh.

'No, hang on, Jimmy lad, the target's mate is moving. He's standing up. Now he's taking off his coat. Now he's sat down again. Right then, my boy, now's your chance.'

Jimmy started climbing to his feet. 'No, wait, he's standing up again.' Beginning to feel like a yoyo, Jimmy gritted his teeth and sat back down, only to notice his former superior had suddenly gone as white as a sheet.

'What's wrong, Sir. You look as if you've seen a ghost.'

'You're not going to believe this, Jimmy, but the bloke Nick Nack's talking to isn't a bloke at all. It's Teddy's mother, Agnes.'

CHAPTER 14

The Japanese detective gives a deep bow as he steps over the threshold. As he straightens, he looks over at Sebastian. 'This is Mr. Sinclair,' I say obligingly. 'He's familiar with the case.'

'I am honoured to make your acquaintance, your grace,' Matsui responds, making it clear he knows exactly who Seb is. He gives another, even deeper bow and for a second, I think he's going to fall over.

'Please, take a seat Mr. Yoshimatsu. Can I get you anything? Tea or coffee?'

'A cup of tea would be very welcome, thank you.' He sits down gingerly as though he thinks we might have boobytrapped the chair.

Five minutes later, I hand him a cup and he takes a sip before looking at me expectantly.

'I will share my findings with you, Mr. Yoshimatsu,' I tell him, my voice carefully polite, 'providing you can assure me of my mother's continued well being and explain exactly what you are doing in Dartmouth.'

He stares at me impassively, and for a moment I think he's not going to answer. Then he sighs abruptly and puts his cup onto the desk.

'I do not know where your mother is,' Ms. Shackleford. 'We had her in our custody up until three days ago when she vanished from our safehouse.'

'Clearly, she didn't feel particularly safe,' I retort. 'Why was she in a safe house in the first place?'

'I believe you are already aware that, until recently, your mother had been the ... err ... *lover* ... of a wealthy Japanese gentleman.'

I nod my head impatiently. 'Do you know who he is?'

'We do, though at present, I am not at liberty to say.'

'Then, we have nothing more to talk about, Mr. Yoshimatsu.' I'm well aware that my response is blunt – in Japanese circles, bloody rude – but I'm done with playing polite games. I stand up to emphasise my point. 'Clearly, I have something you want. But I am not prepared to share anything further with you while you give nothing in return.'

'Your mother is in a great deal of trouble, Ms. Shackleford.' His response is clipped, clearly revealing his frustration.

'We only have your word for that, Mr. Yoshimatsu,' Sebastian interrupts. 'I think you need to tell us what kind of trouble and why.'

For a moment, silence reigns, then abruptly, the detective gives a small nod. 'Please sit down, Ms. Shackleford. I abhor talking to someone's midsection.'

Swallowing my indignant response that I'm not *that* bloody tall, I sink back into my seat.

'Your mother left you thirty years ago, almost to the day, I believe?' I nod and shrug. Not exactly new information. 'I am given to understand you and your father were visited by members of the *Bōryokudan* – *Yakuza* to the Western world.'

'They ransacked the house, but I don't think my father ever knew what they were looking for.'

'They were looking for a pregnancy test,' he responds brusquely. 'Your mother was carrying the child of a very wealthy, very powerful man.'

'How do you know that the baby wasn't my father's?' I say flatly.

He shrugs. 'We don't, or rather we didn't. But clearly her lover believed it was his child.'

'That's why she vanished,' I confirm, 'and why we were told to leave Japan.'

'We believe so, yes.'

'Who is he?'

'His name is Sugana Osamu which I doubt will mean anything to you. And in truth, it is not his birth name, but the one he uses in his business dealings. The one that he uses to generate fear in people.'

'He sounds an all-round nice guy,' I say sarcastically. 'Why did it take my mother thirty years to escape from his clutches? Was she that terrified of him?'

'I think you have misunderstood, Ms. Shackleford. Your mother has never been Sugana's victim. Up until three months ago, she was his willing accomplice.'

I stare at him, completely lost for words. For all my quips about my mother being involved with *Yakuza*, I never for one second *truly* believed her connection with the Japanese mafia had been voluntary.

'What happened three months ago?' Alex asks the question since my voice seems to have seized up.

'Are you aware of the current succession problems facing the Japanese Imperial family?'

'I understand that currently three options are being considered to solve the problem,' Sebastian answers.

'You are correct. The more progressive members of the government favour allowing an Empress to sit on the Chrysanthemum throne. However, the older, more conservative members are strongly against such a move. It is this faction that are pushing for either the reinstatement of the families that lost their royal status after the second world war, or ...'

'... or the current Imperial family could simply adopt all the men from the families who were kicked out provided they are descended from the male-line - which will obviously give them plenty more dicks to choose from - if you'll pardon the pun,' I finish impatiently.

He bends his head but does not comment on my rudeness.

'And I assume Sugana Osamu is a member of one of the former Imperial families?' Sebastian cuts in smoothly. 'Which one does he belong to?'

'I am not at liberty to say,' Matsui repeats, 'but you are correct in your supposition.'

'Is that why he turned on my mother?' I ask in a more even tone. I'm well aware that we'll get nothing out of the detective if I continue with my belligerent tone.

'On the contrary,' he answers. 'It was in fact, the other way round. Your mother *turned on* Sugano.'

This time I stare at him, open mouthed as he continues. 'Your grasp of the succession problem indicates you are aware of the importance of boy children in Japanese society.' He pauses, waiting politely for us to nod. 'The fact that Sugano has a son who is only now reaching thirty years of age is all important to those factions who wish to adhere to the primogenitary rules set in place hundreds of years ago.'

'But what about the fact that the son is both illegitimate and has a non-Japanese mother?' Alex counters.

'These things are easily buried.' Yoshimatsu spreads his hands. 'Birth certificates can be altered if one knows the right people.'

'But what about DNA?' Sebastian asks.

'Again, if the right people are paid off ...' He trails off with a shrug.

'Just a minute,' I interrupt, my voice betraying my frustration. 'This is getting more and more farfetched by the minute. Why on earth would either of them go to such extreme lengths when those in charge might simply decide to allow Imperial Princesses to ascend the throne? If that happens, nobody will care what happens to the defunct members of the family.'

'That may well be true,' he concedes, 'but until the decision is made – and believe me, it could take years – the ...' He pauses and creases his brow. 'How do you say it? The jocking for position will continue.'

'*Jockeying*,' I correct him. 'You say my mother turned on Sugano. Why?'

'To pre-empt him, I believe,' Matsui explains. 'We believe she thought to have him murdered before he had the chance to do the same to her.'

'Bloody hell, it's like the *Wars of the Roses*,' I declare, shaking my head.

'I have seen that movie,' the detective chuckles. 'You are closer than you think, Ms Shackleford. While those who make such decisions continue to argue, both the power and influence of those who stand to rise continues to grow. Your half-brother – Kimuro – Ms Shackleford is one such rising star.'

'But what of his parents' *Yakuza* connections?' Alex asks.

Yoshimatsu spreads his hands and shrugs. 'Those who matter do not give a damn.'

I sit back with a huff. 'So, what do we do? Just let them get on with it?'

I grimace, trying to make sense of it all. 'And what do the pictures have to do with anything? Why did my mother send them to me?'

'My guess is that she didn't,' Matsui responds with a sigh. 'I described Kimuro as a rising star, Ms Shackleford. I did not say he ascends willingly.

'I believe your brother sent the photos to you for safekeeping. But that was not his only reason. He did it to ensure that they did not fall into his parents' hands.'

* * *

'WHAT THE BLOODY hell is Agnes doing in Dartmouth? And with old Nick Nack? When I spoke to him in the pub, he sounded as though he hated her.'

'Perhaps she's come to see Teddy,' Jimmy suggested.

'Then what's she doing skulking around here then? It's not like Teddy's hard to find. You can generally spot her half a mile away.'

Jimmy shook his head, at a complete loss. 'Are you going to speak to her?' he asked instead.

'If I do that, Nick Nack'll know my name's not Jimmy Noon.'

'You told him your name was Jimmy Noon?' Privately, the Admiral thought his friend's outrage was a little over the top.

'Well, I was under cover,' he defended. 'I couldn't give him my name, could I?'

'You gave a Japanese gangster my name?' Jimmy's voice had gone an octave higher, and the Admiral finally realised he might have gone a tad too far.

'I didn't think I'd ever see the bloke again?' he hedged.

'We both know that's complete bollocks, Sir.' Charles Shackleford blinked. His friend hardly ever swore. 'You've been following him around like a fart in a spacesuit since Saturday.'

'I have not,' the Admiral declared indignantly. 'This morning was a complete accident. I had no intention of going anywhere near the bloke.' He said the last with his fingers crossed under the table. Not that he had anything against lying as such, but for some reason, since Boris had popped his clogs, he could have sworn on several occasions that he'd heard the old God Botherer whispering in his ear. It was either that or he needed his ears syringing.

'I have to say, Sir, that I'm very disappointed,' Jimmy was saying. 'The thing is …' Fortunately he was cut off in mid flow as the waiter chose that moment to bring their breakfast.

As they ate, Jimmy listed a dozen different ways the Admiral had disappointed him, while the object of his tirade kept an eye on Nick Nack and Agnes. When the small man ran out of steam after about five minutes, Charles Shackleford was actually quite surprised.

'You're right, lad,' he acknowledged with a dramatic sigh when he was sure Jimmy had finished. 'I can't argue with the truth. The fact is I've simply put far too much on you over the years ...'

'Well, I'm not sure I …'

'… Attributed you with the same cunning intelligence …'

'… I'm certain that's not wha …'

'… The same rank. A fellow brother in arms. A ...' The Admiral paused, mid flow. 'Hang on a minute Jimmy, Nick Nack's just come back from the heads. I don't think we've got long. It's now or never.'

'Now or never for what?' Jimmy asked, frowning at the abrupt change of subject.

'Brown sauce, Jimmy, remember?'

The small man stared at his former superior for a full second, then he sighed and climbed to his feet.

'That's the spirit, Jimmy. Right then, call me when you're in position.'

'Call you, Sir?'

The Admiral gave another pained sigh. 'So, I can hear what they're saying. Make sure to look casual.'

Gritting his teeth, Jimmy began walking towards the couple. Once there, he nonchalantly sauntered along the cereals while surreptitiously looking down at his mobile phone. Unfortunately, after only a couple of seconds, he realised there was no signal. He turned back where he could see the Admiral gesturing urgently towards his phone. Jimmy started to spread his hands in a *what do you want me to do,* gesture but quickly realised he was attracting attention. With a self-conscious cough, he turned back to Nick Nack and Agnes, furtively studying Teddy's mother over the cereal packets.

While she wasn't conventionally pretty by any stretch of the imagination, neither did she resemble a sack of crabs. Her face would best be described as interesting. He could well understand her charisma.

After a second, he realised Agnes was saying something, and stepped a bit closer to listen. Over the top of her head, he could see the Admiral hopping from one foot to the other while alternately pointing his mobile phone in the air and putting it to his ear in a move he'd last seen *John Travolta* perform in *Saturday Night Fever.*

Determinedly focusing his attention on the yoghurts, Jimmy quickly realised that whatever the couple were saying, it wasn't in English. He was just about to give up and return to the table where the Admiral now appeared to be performing a groundbreaking version of *River Dance* watched by a growing crowd of people through the window, when suddenly he heard Agnes say, 'If any harm comes to my daughter, I will kill you.'

CHAPTER 15

'So, if it was my mother who was paying to have Sugano murdered, why did you have her in a safe house?'

'She agreed to give evidence against her former lover in exchange for a deal with the Japanese authorities,' he answers. 'We believed her to be the lesser of two evils. Naturally, Sugano could not allow such a thing. He orchestrated an attack on the house, killing two of our officers, but your mother managed to escape.'

'How did he know where she was?' Alex asks.

Yoshimatsu gives a sigh. 'As I said earlier, Sugano has many in his employ. Police officers too.'

'And you say you do not know where my mother is now?' My voice is harsh, accusing.

'I do not know exactly where she is, no,' he concedes. 'But it is my belief she is here, in Dartmouth.'

'*What?*' I'm completely unable to carry on. I feel as though I've been punched in the gut and want to do nothing more than howl.

'She wants the photographs back. I think the man your uncle spoke with - this *Nick Nack* - is working for her.'

'So, she has her own pet gangsters now,' I declare sarcastically.

'She has her supporters, yes,' he responds carefully.

I feel Seb's steadying hand on my shoulder, and I grit my teeth, fighting the urge to throw it off. The old Teddy wouldn't have hesitated.

'Why would anyone risk their neck to piss off such a powerful man?' he questions.

Yoshimatsu gives a shrug. 'For exactly that reason. There are those who do not wish him to become even more powerful, so they attach themselves to your mother.'

'So, what exactly is so important about these bloody photos?,' I demand.

'Show them to me, and I'll explain.'

Wearily, I give Seb's hand a brief squeeze, then climb to my feet, feeling ridiculously bereft as he lifts his arm from my shoulder. Going to my bag, I pull out the photos and swallow the childish compulsion to fling them at him.

As he takes them from me, his eyes meet mine and I think I detect the briefest flare of sympathy, but it's gone so quickly, I can't be sure it's not in my head.

He takes the pictures out of the envelope and sorts through them, finally choosing the one that shows with my mother holding a baby in her arms, a grim-faced Sugano at her side.

'He doesn't exactly look happy about the prospect of fatherhood,' I comment.

The detective doesn't answer. Instead, he holds the photo towards me, pointing at the house in the background. This building is Megumi

Orphanage. It is the same in all the photos.' I blink, completely confused.

'The child in all of these pictures is your brother, Ms. Shackleford, but he is not Kimuro.

I stare at him, struggling to process what he's telling me. Taking the rest of the photos out of his hand, I sift through them as if somehow the answers will be there. Mr. Yoshimatsu is correct, the building is the same in each one. I'd simply thought it their house. In the final one, the resemblance between the two men is unmistakable. Swallowing a sudden lump in my throat, I hand the pile to Sebastian and look over at the detective.

'What's his name?' I manage.

'Hokama. He was Kimuro's twin.'

'Was?'

'I am sorry to tell you, Ms Shackleford, that Hokama died six months ago.'

Tears spring unbidden to my eyes. How the bloody hell can I cry for someone I never knew existed five minutes ago? 'Why was he in an orphanage?' I feel the word stick in my throat.

'I believe he had a disability - one that his parents wished to keep hidden.'

'So, they sent him to an *institution*?'

Mr. Yoshimatsu sighs. 'Thirty years ago, it was not uncommon in Japan for children with physical or mental disabilities to be separated from their family and sent to childcare institutions.' He gave a small shrug before adding, 'It is still happening now, though thankfully less so.'

'But surely they had the money to pay for childcare at home.' The outrage in Sebastian's voice warms my heart.

'I don't doubt it. But you have to understand that in Japan, there is, even now, shame and social stigma attached to having a child with such problems. Parents will choose to put their children into an institution rather than admitting to their existence publicly or allowing them to be adopted. And since biological parents retain legal custody of their offspring - regardless of whether the infant has been abandoned ...' his voice trails off.

'So, the interests of the parents are put before those of the child?' Alex's voice is disbelieving.

'I am afraid so, though things are gradually changing for the better.'

'So, you're saying that Hokama spent the whole of his life in an institution because his parents were *ashamed* of him?'

Yoshimatsu sighs. 'In this case, it was more than that.'

'Sugano could not be seen to have a son with a disability,' Sebastian guesses. 'Not a good advertisement for a royal bloodline.'

I shake my head in disbelief. I've always known my mother's maternal instincts were paltry at best, but ...

'How does Kimuro fit into all this?' I ask, unwilling to examine my feelings about my mother's callousness.

'He did not discover he had a twin until he was sixteen. I believe he discovered these photos. After that, he insisted on visiting his brother regularly. I understand they became very close.'

'When Hokama died, Kimuro would not allow him to be erased from history. He took the photos, and though Sugano flew into a terrible rage, he refused to reveal where he'd hidden them.'

'You know my brother,' I pronounce, suddenly certain that Kimuro is the real reason Yoshimatsu is in Dartmouth. He doesn't bother to deny it.

'Kimuro is a good man,' he explains simply. 'Nothing like his father.'

'Or his mother,' I add harshly. I shake my head, still struggling to understand the motivations of these unknown people. 'Why the hell did they have a yearly photograph taken with Hokama, if they were trying to forget he existed?'

'The same reason they sent him away,' Yoshimatsu sighs. 'Shame. I'm afraid it still plays far too large a part in my country's culture.'

'So, let me get this straight,' Alex observes. 'Basically, you're saying that both Agnes and Sugano are at each other's throats, vying to manipulate their son who is refusing to be manipulated?'

Yoshimatsu laughs unexpectedly. 'Absurd, is it not?'

'Does he know they're actively trying to kill each other? Alex asks incredulously.

'I think he might actually be grateful if they succeed,' Yoshimatsu responds drily. 'I do not believe he has seen either of his parents for over a year.'

'Are you here on behalf of the NPA or at the behest of my brother?' I ask.

'You are asking whether I am here in an official capacity, then yes, most certainly. My orders are to return your mother to Japan as quickly and discreetly as I can.' He gives his now familiar shrug. 'Kimuro does not wish his mother to cause havoc in your life. I believe he greatly regrets involving you in this unpleasant business by sending the photos to you.'

'Why did he?'

'I think it was a ... how do you say it? A shaking of the knee?'

'A knee jerk reaction,' I supply. Against all the odds, I find myself warming to the diminutive detective.

He gives a small nod, and I can see he's filing the information away for another time.

I have a sudden thought. 'What was in the notebook Mabel found,' I ask, my voice challenging.

He gives a sigh, followed by a wry grin. 'Bookmaker's odds.'

I raise my eyebrows. 'You're kidding.' He shakes his head, and I find myself laughing at the bloody absurdity of it all.

'Do you know why my mother gave an interview with the press?' I ask when I've finished. I'm still mostly baffled by her decision, despite all the conjecture.

'I think perhaps you ...' His words are cut off by a sudden hammering on the door. Startled, we all look over, just as the letterbox pops open and my uncle shouts, 'Teddy, are you in there? You'll never guess who I just bumped into. Did you know your bollocking mother's in Dartmouth?'

BY THE TIME Jimmy got back to their table, the remains of his breakfast were congealing on his plate, though naturally, that didn't pose a problem for Pickles. The crowd watching through the window quickly dispersed when it looked as though their impromptu entertainment had come to an end, and Jimmy had to make do with cold toast while he told the Admiral what he'd overheard.

'I guessed old Nick Nack was a nasty piece of work as soon as I spoke to him,' Charles Shackleford muttered. Then he gripped Jimmy's arm, nearly shoving the last piece of toast up the small man's nostril. 'Don't move, lad, he's coming this way.'

Jimmy froze as Nick Nack stormed past them, a picture of coiled anger. Seconds later he was gone, the door rattling behind him.

'Is Agnes still at the table?' Jimmy asked, not daring to look round. The Admiral nodded.

'And I don't mind telling you when she turned round then, she looked like she'd been chewing a wasp—and that's saying something for Agnes. I think old Nick Nack might have upset her.'

'Do you think we ought to go and talk to her?' Jimmy asked.

Charles Shackleford looked at him askance. 'Have you lost what little sense you were born with, Jimmy? Of course we can't bloody talk to her. If she knows we know she's here, she could do another runner. And then where would we be?'

'On our way home?' the small man suggested wistfully.

'Hang on, Jimmy lad, she's putting her coat on. Get ready, it looks like she's moving.' The Admiral turned sideways in his chair; Pickles' lead wrapped tightly round his hand in preparation for a quick getaway. Jimmy frowned, hoping there wasn't going to be a high-speed chase through the streets of Dartmouth. The last time he'd broken the four-minute mile was on Emily's electric scooter.

After a few seconds when Agnes didn't pass their table, both men dared to look back, just in time to see her following a member of staff up the stairs to the guests bedrooms.

'Quick,' the Admiral hissed. 'We need to find out which room she's stopping in.

'I can tell you now, I'm not pretending to be a cleaner ...'

'Bloody hell, Jimmy you're as spineless as a length of wet spaghetti. I don't know what happened to your sense of adventure.'

'You did, Sir.'

* * *

'I'm really not sure it's a good idea to use the Admiralty to meet a long lost, murderous sister-in-law, Dad.'

135

'I doubt Agnes would do me any harm,' the Admiral chuckled. 'I was her favourite brother-in-law once upon a time.'

'You were her only one,' Tory interjected sourly. 'And, in all honesty, Dad, I've never met anyone who hasn't harboured a secret longing to lamp you one at the very least. Up to and including relatives.'

'Well, what was I supposed to do? Leave 'em to meet on the street?'

'Couldn't they have found a nice cosy cell somewhere?'

Charles Shackleford gave his daughter a shocked look. 'Teddy's family, Victory. I thought she was your friend.'

'She is and I love her,' Tory retorted. 'It's just that Teddy seems to attract trouble to her somehow.'

'I hate to say this Victory, but she's the same as you. It's a Shackleford family trait. And you can't blame her for that bloody fiasco with the strumpet. That was the Scot's fault for not giving the hussy her marching orders when he had the chance.'

'It wasn't Jason's fault,' Tory argued indignantly. Then she sagged and sighed. 'And I know it wasn't Teddy's either. I think I'm just worried, that's all, Dad. These people are dangerous. We've survived one run-in with the criminal underworld, but we might not be so lucky this time round.'

'Agnes is hardly a bloody Mob boss,' the Admiral scoffed.

'That's exactly what she is,' Tory exclaimed. 'According to Teddy's Japanese policeman, she's every bit as bad as the man she ran off with all those years ago. And what about Bill?'

'What about him?' Tory stared at her father in exasperation. He really didn't get it.

'Don't you think he deserves to have a word with her after all this time? Find out why she did a runner, leaving a husband and a seven-year-old daughter?'

The Admiral shook his head. 'No good would come of it, Victory. There are times when it's better to let sleeping dogs lie, and this is one of 'em. If Teddy gets some closure, that's good enough.'

Tory opened her mouth to speak, then shut it again. It always completely threw her when her father spoke actual sense.

'I'm going to have to tell Noah,' she said instead. The Admiral nodded. 'With a bit of luck, he'll tie you to a bloody chair. One of you in the room with Agnes will be quite enough.'

Tory eyed her father narrowly. 'I want to support Teddy, whatever my private thoughts about the wisdom of the whole thing.'

'Since when have you and wisdom appeared in the same sentence? She'll have his Dukeship to cuddle up to,' Charles Shackleford countered bluntly. 'What with Agnes, Yoshiwhateverhisnameis, you, Noah, Jimmy and Uncle Tom bloody Cobley and all, we'll be like sardines. I'm packing Mabel off to bingo.'

'Why is Jimmy coming?'

'Because he's the most sensible one of us all,' her father retorted. 'The one thing you can rely on Jimmy to do is cut through the bollocks and get right to the heart of the matter. And if there are no bollocks tonight, I'm a sumo wrestler's daughter.'

CHAPTER 16

'*I* can't believe I'm actually going to finally meet her again after all this time.' I'm lying on the sofa with my legs scrunched up on Sebastian's knee. Coco is sprawled out on the other sofa, snoring.

'Perhaps you should write a list of questions' he suggests.

'Already done,' I respond with a faint grin. 'This is me you're talking to.'

He reaches down to stroke my hair as I think back to the events after my uncle's shock announcement through the letterbox.

Naturally, our friendly detective became very policemanlike when faced with the prospect of apprehending his quarry. The fact that he was in a foreign country without any backup didn't seem to faze him at all—a man after my own heart, clearly.

Despite my previous experience in the NCA, he asked me not to accompany him, stating that my presence could well make the situation that much more volatile. However, he did promise to allow us time to speak once she was in his custody.

When I asked how he intended to convince her to come quietly, he admitted that my brother had given him a letter. He didn't say what was in it, but it was clear he thought it would be enough to get her to come along without any fuss—especially as she's no longer a British citizen and the authorities here are unlikely to give a toss.

According to my uncle, she's staying at the Bayards Cove Inn, and since Nick Nack apparently stormed off in a bit of a strop half an hour earlier, she was on her lonesome. Room twenty. I didn't ask him how he knew which room she was in…

Evidently, he'd left Jimmy on lookout duty, but urged Yoshimatsu to get a shift on since his former Master at Arms was no longer the man he used to be and was now out of his depth in a car park puddle.

Seconds later they were gone.

'Do you think it's wise to have my uncle present at our first meeting in thirty years?' I quiz Sebastian. I feel I should be nervous, but all I'm feeling at the moment is pissed off that Agnes has caused such upheaval in my life. The seven-year-old child who grieved for her mother is long gone.

'Well, since I'll be there, along with Yoshimatsu, Alex and probably Tory. I think all of us together will be able to prevent you committing grievous bodily harm.'

'It's strange, but I really don't feel much at all. Before I came to Dartmouth, the old me would have been pacing the floor, unable to sit still. It's at times like these that I realise how much I've changed.'

'Why, do you have many long-lost relatives hidden away?' He teases.

'Certainly not ones in the Japanese mafia,' I chuckle. 'I don't think anyway. To be honest, I'm just relieved it's nearly all over.'

'I have to say, you know how to keep a man on his toes,' he returns drily.

We're silent for a while and I close my eyes, enjoying the feeling of his hands massaging my feet.

'Will you come to Scotland for Christmas?' I ask suddenly.

He gives a shrug and my heart plummets like a stone until he says, 'You haven't asked me.'

I frown, thinking back to the last few weeks. 'I'm sure I've mentioned it.'

'Oh, you've mentioned it. You just haven't asked if I want to come with you.'

'Well, I suppose I just thought …' I grind to a halt, suddenly wondering what exactly I had thought. Then I grimace. 'I just sort of assumed you'd be coming,' I finish lamely.

'You know what they say about assumptions.' Seb's voice sounds a little funny and I lift my head to look at him carefully.

'Do you want to come?' I ask levelly. 'If you don't, we could always stay here or at Blackmore.'

'So, you won't go ahead without me, then?'

'Of course not.' My voice is an indignant squeak as I raise myself onto my elbows. 'Unless you've got other plans of course.' I suddenly feel like I've stepped on a hidden minefield. His expression is impassive, but Seb is even better than me at hiding his emotions. 'Have I missed something?' I ask quietly.

He doesn't answer immediately, and my stomach lurches. But then he smiles, and I relax slightly. When did my happiness become so dependent on other people's moods? I stare at his beautiful features and amend my last thought. Not people, *Sebastian*. White hot fear suddenly swamps me at the thought of losing him and I realise that my fatalistic attitude regarding the transitory nature of our relationship left the building ages ago. But I'm nowhere near ready to examine what that means …

When he finally says, 'I'd love to come with you to Bloodstone Tower for Christmas,' I only narrowly avoid shouting, 'Woo-hoo.'

'Will your mother be alright on her own?' I ask instead. His smile turns into a grin at my words.

'Oh, my mother will be fleeing these frozen shores the minute we get into December,' he answers. 'Surely you remember last Christmas?'

I think back. Last Christmas, Sebastian had been organising the first Christmas house party at Blackmore Grange. I'd politely declined his invitation - I think I said something along the lines of, 'I'd rather have my tongue cut out than make small talk to fifty complete strangers' - and I spent the day over at Tory and Noah's instead. I give a small internal grin. She'd just given birth to the twins, and spent the whole day reclining on the sofa, while the rest of us ran around like headless chickens. I remember the Christmas dinner had been lovely, though according to Freddy, it was precisely because Tory hadn't actually cooked it. I couldn't really argue as my only experience of her culinary skills had been during *Operation Strumpet* as the Admiral still insists on calling it ...

'I thought she was with you at Blackmore.'

He gives me a horrified look. 'I try very hard not to put my mother and our hotel guests together in the same room. We'd be broke if I did. No, I think last year she went to Barbados.'

I can't help smiling at the thought of his mother indulging in her version of polite conversation, sporting a tiara and different coloured shoes. 'Very nice. Where's she off to this year?'

'This year it's Thailand. I think Roger's keen to have an authentic Thai massage. How about your father?'

'Delia next door,' I answer promptly wiggling my eyebrows. 'If you come to Scotland, who will run this year's Christmas house party?'

'It's Simon, my hotel manager's turn.'

'Won't the guests be disappointed you're not there doing your whole *Dinner with the Duke* thing?'

'Simon's every bit as good at shmoozing the guests – better actually, because he doesn't have the inherent rudeness that all of us with a title are born with.'

'Ah, so you acknowledge it then?'

'Of course. It's why we dinosaurs still exist. Got to keep the commoners in their place.'

'Not many dukes indulge in feet rubbing then,' I quip, poking my toe up his nose. He rears back laughing before shaking his head in mock horror.

'You have no idea how privileged you are.'

'I suppose I'll just have to find a way to express my gratitude then,' I murmur, pulling the same foot back and rubbing it just where I know it will be most effective. His indrawn breath is my reward, and I immediately feel an answering tightness.

'Have we got enough time for you to express your gratitude properly?' His voice is already hoarse.

'It'd be my pleasure, yer grace,' I respond with a wink. "ow could a lowly maid like me refuse such an 'andsome gent a good priggin'…'

* * *

DID I say I wasn't nervous? Well, that might have been the case a couple of hours ago, but right now, I wish I was anywhere but the Admiralty.

Fortunately, Tory is on hand with a fortifying glass of wine. 'Who's looking after Isaac and the twins?' I ask.

'Did you ever meet Kit's Aunt Flo?'

I frown and shake my head. 'I don't think so.'

'Oh well,' she grins, 'you're in for a treat at Christmas. She writes bonkbusters for a living. Kit and I learned everything we know about sex from her books.'

'And you're leaving your children with her?' I ask in mock horror.

'I'm hoping all I need to do is hand Tobi and Ember a copy of *Fierce Sweet Surrender* as soon as they're old enough and that'll be me done.'

I can't help but laugh. Tory is the perfect *imperfect* mother. She gives the rest of us hope.

Before I can ask her to repeat the title of the book, a loud buzzing sound puts a stop to all conversation. With a quick squeeze of my shoulder, Tory follows her father to the intercom. 'IS THAT YOU YOSHI?' he yells. I wince at the nickname, my apprehension at having the Admiral present rising a notch.

'I see your manners haven't improved any, Charlie Shackleford.' My heart slams against my chest as I hear my mother's voice for the first time in thirty years.

Ten minutes later, eight of us are lined up opposite each other – four to a sofa. It feels as though we're waiting for a bus. The only two missing are Tory and Noah, who, in time honoured British tradition, are currently making tea. Naturally, there were a few dubious looks cast their way with Noah hailing from across the Pond, but I can vouch for the fact that he's taken to such British traditions like a duck to water. His current tea bag of choice is *Lidl's* own, much to Freddy's disdain.

Of course, the Japanese are almost as obsessed with tea drinking as we are, but Tory told me she'd decided against getting any in specifically for our oriental guest after the Admiral announced the stuff tasted like the inside of a sumo wrestler's jock strap. He doesn't need any additional help in being offensive.

So far, I've managed to avoid my mother's gaze. She's sitting close enough to Yoshimatsu that one could be forgiven for thinking they're an item. Suddenly, I just want the whole thing to be over so I can get on with my life.

As Tory and Noah return with the tea and biscuits – fortunately, our three canine friends have been relegated to my uncle's study to avoid the whole situation becoming more farcical that it already is – I finally allow my eyes to meet my mother's. If I was hoping to see any remorse, it only takes a few seconds for me to realise there is no regret in their depths.

'You are looking well, Teddy,' she says carefully. Somehow, her use of my nickname sets my teeth on edge.

'I am well, thank you' I manage. God, this is excruciating. We'll be here all bloody day at this rate. Yoshimatsu is allowing me this time with her as a favour – so I can ask the questions that have been haunting me. So, I just need to bloody well *ask* them.

Taking a deep breath, I school my expression into one of indifference. 'Why did you give the newspaper interview?' She blinks, and I can tell she's surprised at the question.

In the end, she gives a shrug. 'I wanted you to know I was still alive. I didn't know at the time that Kim intended to send you the photos, but I was afraid I might have to leave Japan in a hurry.'

It takes me a second to realise that the Kim she's referring to is Kimuro. A sudden flash of resentment envelopes me and Sebastian, ever tuned to my moods, takes my hand in a tight grip. All those elaborate reasons I made up for her actions – and I couldn't have been more wrong. She just thought she might need a bolt hole if everything went tits up.

'Why did my brother send the photos to me?' I ask. Her lips tighten at my use of the word brother, and I feel a petty sense of triumph.

'He did not wish them to fall into his father's hands,' she says at length.

'Neither did he wish them to fall into yours,' Yoshimatsu comments mildly. 'You did not come here for sanctuary; you came to take the photos from your daughter – preferably without her knowing.'

'Does your Japanese friend know you've been caught?' I ask, trying hard to keep my voice impassive.

'I have not been *caught*,' she retorts. 'Neither have I reneged on the agreement I made with the NPA. The photos belong to me as Hokama's mother.'

'You mean the child you abandoned?' I shoot back. 'Getting to be a habit, Mother.'

She narrows her eyes at me but doesn't respond and suddenly my dig just sounds vindictive. I bite my lip, fighting to regain my calm. I know she's waiting for me to ask why she left me. But since I found out about Hokama, I realise it was actually nothing personal - she's always done whatever was expedient for her at the time. Self-centred doesn't even begin to describe my mother.

And I suddenly realise something else. Leaving when she did was the best gift she could have given me.

There is nothing more to say. By giving evidence against her former lover and Kimuro's father, my mother has condemned herself to a life in the shadows. I have no doubt Sugano will have people looking for her - even from prison. And she's lost whatever control she had over my brother.

She has nobody.

I look over at Matsui Yoshimatsu. 'Do you have everything you need?'

He gives a shrug. 'Well, Shirai Tadao - Nick Nack - is still free, but I am certain he will return to Japan, once he recognises, he is alone here. When he does, he will find a welcoming committee at the airport.'

I look round at my companions. At the end of the day, they haven't needed to intervene at all. The only thing they've had to provide is their silent support.

And suddenly I understand that that was the only reason they came.

CHAPTER 17

*A*s I watch Yoshimatsu direct my mother into the car and drive away, I feel as though a tremendous weight has been lifted off my shoulders. Turning to Seb, elation bubbling up inside me, I'm surprised to see concern in his eyes. I lean into him and kiss him fiercely. 'I'm fine,' I say, laying my palm against his cheek. 'No, actually, I'm better than fine ... or I will be when I've had a drink.'

He accepts my reassurance with a relieved smile and lays his arm across my shoulders, directing me back into the Admiralty, where Noah is already opening a bottle of wine.

'I reckon old Agnes might well be having a facelift in the not-too-distant future,' my uncle predicts in his usual inimitable fashion. 'Either that or she'll have to find herself a bloody desert island. From what I can gather, her ex is not the forgiving kind.'

'Bloody hell, Dad,' Tory protests, mouthing *sorry* to me over his head, 'can't you occasionally be a little more considerate of other people's feelings?'

'If you're talking about Teddy,' he retorts as if I'm not just standing two feet away, 'I reckon she'll be thinking the same as the rest of us – makes no bloody sense to keep hauling on a fouled anchor.'

'I'll drink to that,' I say, holding up my glass and gripping Seb's hand tightly. 'Seriously, I want to say thank you to every one of you for being here today. But not just that - you're the reason my life is as amazing as it is.' My voice actually breaks slightly as I add, 'Thank you for taking me in. I can truly say I've never been so happy.'

'Don't say another word,' Alex orders grimly, holding out his hand. For a second, I look at him in confusion. 'If Freddy so much as gets a whiff of emotional baggage shedding while he's not here, my life won't be worth living …'

* * *

'The one thing I don't understand, Jimmy, is that bloke, what's his face - Tado …Tadi …Tada …, oh bollocks, *Nick Nack*.'

'What about him, Sir?'

'His comments about Agnes for a start. I don't care what anybody says, you don't put on that kind of bloody animosity.'

Although *Operation Nick Nack* was over, the Admiral had suggested he and Jimmy meet in the Ship for a spot of a post operation analysis. Jimmy had no problem with that, especially as Emily had gone off with Mabel to their weekly Rummikub group, and there was nothing on the telly. Of course, if it had been up to him, he'd have declared the entire operation a perfect example of a self-adjusting cock-up and left it at that.

Jimmy sipped his pint thoughtfully. For once, he couldn't argue with his former superior's reasoning. The Admiral's track record for seeing conspiracies in the bottom of a bag of pork scratchings was legendary, but in this case, Jimmy thought his friend had a point. He thought back to Agnes's threat if her accomplice made the mistake of hurting her daughter. 'You reckon she was going to use Nick Nack to get those photos back off Teddy?' he asked.

The Admiral narrowed his eyes and steepled his fingers in true Holmesian fashion, though it was somewhat ruined by the ketchup covered chip he was holding between his forefinger and thumb.

'I would have thought that was precisely her intention, Jimmy lad. And I have to say she gave up the idea of nabbing 'em pretty bloody sharpish when old Yoshi turned up.' He bit the top off his chip before waving it at the small man, adding, 'And what about the way Nick Nack stormed out of the Bayards? What was all that about?'

'She couldn't see his face though could she, Sir.' Jimmy had a sudden feeling of disquiet. 'What happened to the photos, Sir? Did Mr Yoshi-matsu take them with him?'

After a second, the Admiral frowned and shook his head. 'He said they'd be safer here. He told Teddy to put 'em somewhere safe while he took a set of copies back to Japan with him.'

The two men stared at each other.

'Are you thinking what I'm thinking, Sir?'

'Old Nick Nack's still after the photos.'

'But who's he after them for...?'

* * *

I'M WELL aware that Seb has got to go back to Blackmore. This week's *Dinner with the Duke* is only two days away and he can only miss it under extreme circumstances like death.

And now the danger is over, there's no longer any reason for him to stay. The problem is – I don't want him to go. It's as simple as that.

The last couple of days the weather has taken a turn for the worse and by the time I reach the steps leading up to the garden, the drizzle has turned to full-blown horizontal rain. Dusk settles around me like a shroud as I start up the steep steps, my head tucked down into my coat. Halfway up, I can see the lights from the Boathouse and the warm feeling of expectation and longing hits me like a sledgehammer.

How on earth will I cope if Sebastian does decide I'm not Duchess material? I stop, my heart thudding erratically in my chest. Would I marry him if he asked me? I stare back through the driving rain down at the lights on the river. It's the first time I've allowed myself to seriously consider marriage to Seb. Up until now, I've shoved the thought away whenever it popped up.

I'm well aware that under all the glitziness, marriage to a peer of the realm is not for the fainthearted and I repeat my internal well-worn mantra – I'm hardly duchess material.

I know I'm getting wet, but I can't seem to make myself move. I think back to our recent conversations. To Seb asking me if I wanted to move in. I told him to ask me again once the mess with my mother was over. Well, it's over now.

But what if he doesn't ask me? Do I take the bull by the horns and inform him that I'm now ready to take the next step? I start climbing again. The old Teddy would have been packing up her things round about now. Before coming to Dartmouth, soul searching was a seventies band. I never wanted to look that deeply into myself. But since coming here – and even more so since my mother crashed briefly back into my life – I seem to be spending most of my time in my bloody head.

As I reach the top and start up the garden path, I grit my teeth. I have to stop dithering. The one thing about the old Teddy was that she never, *ever*, prevaricated. If there was something she wanted, she'd take steps to get it. It was as simple as that.

Well, now I want Sebastian. I want to live with him forever. And I want to be his wife. There, I've said it. All I have to do now is tell him – well, the first part at least.

I turn off the main path towards the welcome lights of my little home, warm anticipation replacing fear and uncertainty. I'll tell him I want to move in as soon as get inside -before I lose my nerve. By the time I grasp the door and push, I'm actually smiling to myself, but just as I step inside, his name already on my lips, I stumble to a halt, taking in the unbelievable scene in front of me.

Seb is standing next to the table, gripping the back of a chair. His eyes are on my face, desperation warring with anger and fear. I can hear whining and scratching coming from the bathroom, but I barely register it. My complete attention is taken by the gun currently pressed to the side of Sebastian's head.

'I have come for the photographs, Ms Shackleford. If you do not give them to me, I will blow the back of his head off.'

* * *

'I THINK you should call Teddy, Sir.' For once, the Admiral didn't argue, but simply nodded and fumbled for his phone. Seconds later he muttered, 'Bollocks,' as the answerphone kicked in. Cutting the call, he tried again. When the same thing happened, he looked up at Jimmy, his expression alternating between excitement and uncharacteristic panic.

'Have you got the Duke's number?' Jimmy asked. The Admiral shook his head and tried Teddy's number again. Still no answer. This time, he left a message. 'Bollocking hell, Teddy, answer the bloody phone. Call me back – it's urgent.'

'I think we should call the police, Sir,' Jimmy declared.

'And tell them what? That a murderous Japanese gangster with a mouthful of gold teeth may or may not be trying to forcibly obtain some incriminating photos from a friend?'

'It doesn't sound very plausible when you put it like that.' Jimmy conceded.

'And by the time the police get here, it'll likely all be done and dusted with Nick Nack boarding the next bloody plane to Japan.'

The small man nodded, then found himself saying the very words he'd sworn to Emily he'd never again utter without her standing next to him. 'I think we're going to have to investigate, Sir.'

The two men quickly downed their pints and hurried to the door. They were both like coiled springs – well, second hand ones anyway. Even Pickles picked up on the nervous excitement and was right at their heels as they stepped out into the gathering dusk.

'We'll go straight down to the Lower Ferry,' the Admiral decided. 'There's no point fetching the car. We could be halfway to Daphers' place by the time we've got it started.' He tried Teddy's phone again as they trotted down the road to the ferry slip, but it just went to the answerphone again.

Fortunately, there was a ferry waiting at the slip, just getting ready to leave.

As the two men and Pickles squeezed their way past the cars to the front, Jimmy had a sudden idea. 'Do you have Daphne Sinclair's number, Sir?' he asked.

'Why the bloody hell would I have Daphers' number?' Charles Shackleford answered irritably.

'I'm sure Emily has it. I'll give her a call now.' Seconds later he was reassuring his wife that he wasn't actually having an affair with the batty widow, because if he was, at the very least he'd have her number. 'Is Charlie with you?' she said then. Jimmy winced as the Admiral shook his head violently while running his finger backwards and forwards across his throat.

'Err... yes,' Jimmy admitted, much to his former superior's frustration. 'We're just trying to get hold of Teddy, but she's not answering her phone.' The Admiral looked on in horror, mouthing, 'now you've gone and bloody done it.'

'No, he just wanted to tell her that she left her ... err ... *scarf* at the Admiralty the other day.' He paused to give a thumbs up sign before adding, 'I think it's a very expensive one – a gift from his grace.' By this point, the Admiral could see that Jimmy was sweating a bit. They were approaching the Dartmouth slipway and any second now, Emily was going to hear the bang as the ferry landed. 'No dearest, it's just that he didn't want Teddy to worry.' Jimmy's voice was definitely cracking with the strain and Charles Shackleford fought the urge to snatch the phone off him. Bloody hell, he was definitely going to have to share a few tips on telling a convincing porker. 'Love you too,' Jimmy all but shouted, cutting the call just seconds before the ferry hit the bottom of the slip with a resounding boom.

A moment later, there was a ping as Daphne Sinclair's contact details came through.

'I'll give Teddy one last try before we give Daphers a go,' the Admiral was saying as they cut up the steps from Bayards Cove towards Southtown. After a few seconds, he shook his head. 'Right then, give me Daphers' number.'

'Is that you Daphne?' he asked moments later. A pause, then, 'No, I'm not trying to sell you anything. It's Admiral Shackleford. Another pause. 'No, I'm not from the Gas Board. It's *Admiral Shackleford*.' He covered the mouthpiece up and shook his head. 'Deaf as a bloody doorknob.

'THAT'S RIGHT, *CHARLIE SHACKLEFORD*, TEDDY'S UNCLE. I'M TRYING TO GET HOLD OF HER BUT SHE'S NOT ANSWERING HER PHONE, AND I WAS WONDERING IF YOU'D SEEN HER.' After a few seconds, the Admiral turned to Jimmy. 'She says lights are on in the Boathouse.'

'NO, I DON'T THINK IT'S A GOOD IDEA FOR YOU TO GO AND CHECK.' He covered the phone again. 'Bloody hell, Jimmy, that's all we need, the dowager Duchess of Blackmore being held hostage by a Japanese lunatic.'

'DAPHNE? DAPHERS? ARE YOU THERE?' He finally tucked the phone back into his pocket and turned to Jimmy in despair. 'Bloody daft woman's gone down to check. Come on, Jimmy lad, there's no time to lose.'

CHAPTER 18

*D*aphne Sinclair had another quick look through the window, then resumed making herself a gin and tonic. The weather was filthy. Did she really want to go out in it?' Then she held up the bottle. Nearly empty. The only one she had left in the cupboard was that dreadful stuff she'd won at the last Ladies Afloat raffle – the one that tasted like Polish mouthwash. She looked over at the twinkling windows of the Boathouse. Even if she didn't have *Hendricks*, Teddy was almost certain to have a brand that didn't clean one's teeth at the same time – especially while Sebastian was staying there.

She popped a slice of cucumber and a couple of cubes of ice into her glass and sipped it thoughtfully. Why was Charlie Shackleford trying to get hold of Teddy? Could it be something to do with her mother? It was Mabel, after all, who'd let it slip about Agnes Shackleford's connection with the Japanese Underworld. Daphne took another sip. She hadn't spent much time with Sebastian while he was here, and since Friday was looming, he'd likely be heading back to Blackmore – perhaps even tomorrow. It wouldn't do any harm to pop in for a quick chat before dinner.

Her mind made up, Daphne went into the hall, and placed her drink on a side table while she put on her mac. Then, with an umbrella in one hand and a gin and tonic in the other, she ventured out into the rain.

* * *

'WHAT MAKES you think I have the photos here?' I ask levelly, playing for time. My heart was galloping, but I determinedly tuned out everything but my next move. I'd been trained for circumstances like this. I don't look at Seb again but keep my eyes firmly on his captor. Even so, I'm aware that his hands are secured behind his back.

'Where else could they be?' he sneers. 'A safe deposit box perhaps? Except that I cannot imagine there are many such things in Dartmouth.'

'Did my mother tell you to take them from me?' I quiz him. 'I understand she warned you about hurting me.' I'm not sure whether it's wise of me to remind him, but as long as I can keep him talking ...

'She said nothing about your friends.' He shoved the barrel of the gun viciously against Seb's head. 'And who says I'm working for that bitch anyway?' My mind whirls, inconsistencies suddenly clicking into place. My uncle mentioned this man's dislike for my mother. He was working for Sugano. Of course he was. I grit my teeth, irrationally angry at Yoshimatsu for failing to see that Shirai Tadao was working both sides.

'Agnes Shackleford is giving evidence against your boss,' I remind him. 'The photos won't make any difference to that.'

'It will be many months before it comes to trial.' He grins and I can see what my uncle meant about the number of gold teeth in his mouth - not ideal if he's looking to blend in. 'She could quite easily have an accident before then.'

'My stomach roils. She might not be my favourite person, but I would still prefer it if my mother lived healthy but miserable into a ripe old age.

'The Japanese authorities will be waiting for you as soon as you set foot in Japan,' I tell him.

'I am not afraid of them,' he scoffs. 'Osamu Sama will soon take his rightful place in the Imperial family and his son will cease his youthful foolishness.' I really have to admire his optimism.

'Enough,' he shouts abruptly, making me jump. *'Photographs, now.'* His face is cold and set and I recognise that he'll allow no more dissembling. Gritting my teeth, I make my way past the dividing screen to the bedroom area. 'Stay where I can see you,' he orders, dragging Sebastian around.

'The photos are on the top shelf,' I throw back. 'So, unless you come in with me, you will not be able to see what I'm doing.' Clearly, he thinks I might have a weapon stashed away. I wish…

I wait for a second for him to decide what to do. There certainly isn't enough room in the tiny bedroom for all three of us. And he might lose control of his hostage. The scratching and whining gets louder from the bathroom.

'Do not do anything stupid,' he snaps. 'I have a gun to his head, and I *will* shoot him.'

I feel sweat break out on my forehead. Even if I did have a gun, I'd be unable to use it in time. Tadao holds all the cards. In that second, I finally accept that I have to give the photos to him. What the hell does it matter anyway? My mother is in the custody of the Japanese police – she's their problem now. And as for Japanese succession. Sugano can be the next bloody emperor as far as I'm concerned. A bunch of photos are not worth risking Sebastian's life for.

Climbing onto a small stool, I stretch up to a cupboard, high on the wall, my fingers reaching for the envelope I know I put in there just days ago. Unfortunately, my fingers are simply groping fresh air. The envelope is gone.

* * *

'OLD DAPHERS COULD DO with a bloody chair lift to get up here,' the Admiral wheezed, pausing to hold on to a convenient rock. 'Is it me or is the air a bit thinner?'

'I don't think we've got much further to go, Sir,' Jimmy panted, a bit puffed himself. 'I can see the outline of the boathouse from ...' He paused and craned his neck into the gloom. 'Has Teddy put her Christmas decorations up do you know?'

'I wouldn't have thought she'd have had the bloody time, what with murderous Japanese gangsters and what not. Why?'

'Well, I can see something on the Boathouse roof. I can't quite make it out and I was wondering if it was one of those big floaty Santas you see everywhere now.' He narrowed his eyes and frowned. 'Mind you, it looks more like one of those elves on a shelf that are all the rage. Our youngest granddaughter loves 'em. Bit of a pain for the parents though. Our Mandy's husband put the last one they had through the shredder. Mandy told him he needed therapy.'

'What are you on about, Jimmy? I doubt very much that Teddy has a bollocking elf on her roof.' He turned round and peered towards the Boathouse. He said nothing for a few seconds, then 'You're right, Jimmy there is something up there, but it looks more like Rumpelstilt-skin than a bloody elf.

'I can't imagine Teddy would want Rumpelstiltskin on her roof. Not very Christmassy.'

As they watched, whatever it was began to slide ever so slowly towards the edge of the roof. 'I hope she's tied it on properly,' Jimmy commented as the legs went over the side.

'All of a sudden, a faint, '*Hello,*' came drifting towards them. 'Talking elves, whatever will they think of next,' Jimmy chuckled to Pickles as they resumed their climb.

'Bit of a waste of time in this weather,' the Admiral added. 'I mean no-one's likely to hear it. Batteries are bloody expensive and an elf that size must take at least half a dozen.'

'*Hello,*' came again.

'You'd have thought with all the technology nowadays, the bloody thing would say a bit more than *hello,*' the Admiral grunted as they finally reached the top.

'*Is that you, Charlie?*'

'Well, that's clever,' Jimmy declared. 'Do you think it's got some kind of sensor?'

'*I think I might be a little stuck, so if you could grab hold of my legs, it would be most appreciated.*' The two men were rooted to the spot in awestruck silence.

'*Are you deaf, intoxicated, or simply stupid?*'

The Admiral frowned and took a few steps forward. 'Bloody hell, it's Daphers,' he breathed incredulously.

'*Bravo, I knew you'd get there in the end. Could you just stand on that rock and take this off me?*' Wondering if he was somehow hallucinating, Charles Shackleford stepped onto the rock she indicated and held up his hand. Seconds later, she handed him a large gin and tonic before carefully slipping the rest of the way off the roof. Then she dusted off her mac and took the glass of him.

'Right then, Charlie Shackleford, I think we have a teensy problem,' she murmured.

'Only one,' he managed faintly as Jimmy came up with Pickles, fully convinced he'd drunk a bad pint.

'I feel I should warn you that Sebastian and Teddy are being held at gunpoint inside.'

Both men looked incredulously towards the Boathouse.

'What the bloody hell were you doing on the roof?' Charles Shackleford asked her after a second.

'You might notice that the curtains are actually closed,' she answered taking a sip of her drink. 'Bugger, the cucumber's gone soft.' She sighed and added, 'I was simply doing a recce through the only window I knew I'd be able to see through.'

'How come they didn't hear you?' Jimmy questioned her doubtfully.

'Darling, I had this little chalet built for couples. And since I had no wish to intrude upon any weekend fantasies they might wish to enact. I had both the roof, and the walls reinforced for extra privacy. One could hang from the ceiling dressed as The Lone Ranger shouting, *Hi-Yo Silver* at the top of one's voice and anyone standing right outside the front door would be completely oblivious.'

The Admiral shook his head, trying to concentrate on the important bit. 'You say Teddy and Sebastian are being held hostage by a gun wielding madman?' he grilled her.

'Well, in fairness, I didn't describe him as a gun wielding anything. But I think that probably sums it up quite nicely.'

'Bloody hell, it's got to be Nick Nack,' the Admiral groaned to Jimmy. 'We were too bloody slow, lad.'

Daphne frowned, but didn't ask any questions, much to the Admiral's relief. Thank God she wasn't Mabel or Emily.

She did, unfortunately ask what the plan was, adding, 'When I looked through the skylight, I could see your Nick Nack holding a gun to my poor Sebastian's head. Teddy looked very serious, I have to say.'

'Well, having a gun held to your boyfriend's head is hardly cause for a bollocking celebration,' the Admiral growled. 'What a bloody cake and arse party.'

'Quite,' she murmured, nodding.

'I'm not sure how we're going to disarm him,' Jimmy added worriedly, he's probably very good at Jujitsu or something.'

'So am I darling, so don't worry your little head about that. What we need is a distraction. Something to make him point his gun away from my son's head. By the way, what exactly is the blackguard after? Is it something to do with that package I delivered to Teddy last week?'

The Admiral had no idea but thought it likely.

'Should I simply knock at the door?' Daphne suggested. 'I mean after all, it's not beyond the realm of possibility that I might pop in.'

'It might distract him,' the Admiral mused thoughtfully, 'but then, it might also make him pull the trigger.' He pursed his lips and thought for a second. 'What we need is a two-pronged attack. One of us on the roof and one of us at the door. I mean, he can't look in two places at once, so one of us might get a chance to overpower him.'

'Whoever's positioned at the skylight can hopefully warn Teddy off,' Jimmy suggested. 'That's if she's facing the right way of course.'

The Admiral narrowed his eyes and nodded. 'Right then, I'll go up, and once I'm in position, you knock on the door, Daphers.'

'What do you want me and Pickles to do?' Jimmy asked.

'Second line defence. Don't let the bugger get away.' Glancing at the curtained window, he hurried over to the same rock he'd stepped on earlier. 'But first, you need to give me a leg up.'

'They're not there,' I tell Tadeo, my cool as a cucumber façade stretched to breaking point.

He stares at me in silence for a full thirty seconds. 'You're lying,' he spits out eventually.

I shake my head, beginning to lose my temper. 'Why the hell would I lie? You think I would risk my … friend's life for a few poxy photographs?' I grit my teeth, clenching my hands so hard my finger-nails dig into my palms. 'My mother must have taken them. Clearly, she didn't trust you, and, well … you know where I live, so, she must have known too.' Truthfully, I have no idea how Agnes managed to find the time to come up here. I know my voice is getting louder, but for some reason, I'm struggling to hold it together. I risk a look at Sebastian and want to weep at the love and trust in his eyes.

Tadeo is beginning to unravel, I can feel it. And it terrifies me. All this over a few bloody pictures. I raise my face to the roof, reaching for some semblance of calm, when all of a sudden, through the skylight window, I see a large swollen protuberance pressed against the glass. As it suddenly blinks, I swallow the urge to scream, my eyes frantically trying to make sense of the unknown horror that's currently crouched on the Boathouse roof.

Then, just as I'm about to start hyperventilating, there's a knock on the door.'

Things happen very quickly after that. As Tadeo instinctively glances towards the door, Sebastian swiftly turns his head towards the gang-ster and lunges to the side, his forehead connecting with his captor's sensitive earlobe. With a howl, Tadeo loosens his grip, and as I watch Sebastian begin to overbalance, his hands still tied behind his back, I automatically jump forward, my arm pulled back, fingers clenched, ready to hammer my fist into the bastard's face. At the same time, Tadeo turns his head, stares directly at me, then lifts up the hand holding the gun and fires.

I feel a blinding pain in my right shoulder and stumble forward, my vision darkening at the edges. Abruptly the floor rushes up to meet me and everything goes black.

CHAPTER 19

I'm not sure whether it's the lights or the pain in my shoulder that finally wakes me. For a second, I wonder where the hell I am, and then the memories come flooding back. Lifting my head in sudden panic, I immediately let it drop back with a gasp as the pain becomes agony. I must have made a noise, because abruptly a shadow covers the light above my head. Sebastian. 'You're awake.' His voice is low, and I realise it's the early hours of the morning.

'So are you,' I rasp. 'Is there any water?' He nods, picks up a glass and lifts my head again, this time gently and just enough for me to sip the tepid liquid. Once my mouth no longer feels as though it has a dead rodent in it, I lay my head back with a sigh as he pulls up a chair.

'The bastard bloody well shot me,' I mutter. 'I hope you got him.'

Sebastian nods. 'Pickles brought him down as he tried to run.'

'What the hell was Pickles doing there?'

'He wasn't the only one. It seems as though the Admiral, Jimmy and my mother joined forces to rescue us.'

I give a sudden gasp, remembering the dreadful *thing* I saw through the skylight. As I try to describe it, Sebastian abruptly laughs out loud. 'It was your uncle,' he divulges when he finally gets his mirth under control. 'Apparently he was supposed to give you a heads up that the cavalry were on their way.'

I find myself smiling with him. 'How did Pickles save the day?'

'As soon as the gun went off, my mother, bless her, came storming in, yelling like a banshee. She was loud enough that he probably thought that she was leading an army. Basically, he panicked and ran.'

'She wasn't hurt, was she?' I ask, already imagining the next edition's headlines.

He shook his head. 'He shoved her out of the way and fortunately, she fell into the sofa. He headed straight for Jimmy and Pickles – I can only assume he didn't see them. All Jimmy had to do was stick out his foot, and the bastard crashed headlong into the rockery. I'm not quite sure whether it was Pickles who finally finished him off, or my mother's laughing Buddha.'

'Is my uncle okay?'

Sebastian laughs again. 'Not a scratch on him, though he wasn't very happy about having to sit on the roof until we managed to find a ladder.'

I move my arm, and my shoulder gives an answering throb. 'So, do we have matching bullet wounds now?' I quip, turning my head to eye the bandage.

'Almost,' he answers, his voice unexpectedly serious. I look at him with raised eyebrows.

'Am I about to get a lecture?'

He stares at me, and for a split second his eyes echo the terror he must have felt as he watched me fall to the floor. Then he sighs, running his fingers through his hair, leaving it delightfully mussed. I suddenly realise just how tired he must be and lay my good arm on his. 'You need to sleep,' I murmur. 'You can't sit here all night.'

'I already have,' he retorts with a weary grin. 'Dawn's about an hour away.'

'Go home, Seb.' I give his arm a little push. 'Thank you for staying with me.' My voice cracks a little, and he takes my hand, gripping it as though he never wants to let it go.

'I thought I'd lost you,' he says hoarsely.

'I'm not so easy to kill,' I joke as he raises my hand to his lips.

'From now on, I'm never letting you out of my sight again.'

'There are some things that really shouldn't be shared,' I quip. He shakes his head at me, holding my hand against his chest. My breath hitches as I stare up at him.

'Don't joke,' he whispers. 'Losing you would finish me, Teddy.' I stare at him in wonder. How the bloody hell had I managed to win the heart of someone like Sebastian Sinclair? I still can't quite believe it.

'I suppose I'd better move in with you, then.'

'Not enough.' My heart slams against my ribs as I dare to hope.

He drops my hand and braces himself on the bed before bending forward, closer and closer, until his lips cover mine in a mind drugging kiss. When he finally raises his head, he whispers, 'Will you marry me, Teddy?'

I manage a nod through the sudden lump in my throat, and his answering smile is blinding. Then he kisses me again...

* * *

THE NEXT THREE days pass in a blur of visitors - both human and canine - and chocolates. Lots of chocolates. According to the Admiral, old Nick Nack was shipped back to Japan as soon as they realised the rash covering his face was not from internal bleeding, but the patch of poison ivy he'd fallen into.

Mr. Yoshimatsu called too, asking after my welfare. Unfortunately, he was unable to shed any light on the missing pictures, and my mother flatly denies having them. He didn't seem overly upset, proclaiming that, 'Fortune and misfortune come alternatively.' I've come to the conclusion that the Japanese are a very pragmatic race.

It's strange to think I have a half-brother over the other side of the world that I'll likely never meet. But then, what would be the point? I know from experience that blood is not thicker than water. Kimuro is a stranger to me. The only thing we have in common is a shared birth mother.

On the day before I'm due to be discharged, Tory comes in with some good news. 'Kit's had a boy,' she announces, her voice brimming with delight.

I instinctively go to clap my hands, then wince. 'Are they both okay? I thought you knew she was having a boy.'

She nods, helping herself to a chocolate. 'Mother and baby are doing fine. The labour was like shelling peas, apparently. However, she was moaning that no one warned her about the chronic physical torture that is breast feeding. She said it was like having her nipples in a grinder.'

I wince. 'Has she sent you any photos?'

She grins and pulls out her phone, holding it out for me to see. 'Meet Hugo Angus Buchannan. Doesn't he look like his dad?' I look at the screaming, red-faced baby in the picture and have to fight the urge to laugh. 'The absolute image,' I agree.

The following day, Sebastian comes to collect me from Torbay hospital. While I'm certain he would prefer to move me lock, stock and barrel into Blackmore, I need time to prepare myself before becoming lady of the manor. So, we agree that we'll both stay in Dartmouth until the wedding is arranged and our engagement announced to everyone who needs to know. Which appears to be a surprisingly large number of people.

Coco of course is ecstatic to see me, and Daphers too is surprisingly watery-eyed when she comes round with a bottle of bubbly. 'I didn't want to get you more chocolates sweetie, she declares, kissing the air on either side of my face. 'The ones you've eaten already have made you fat enough and everyone knows Champagne is a laxative ...'

She seems perfectly happy with the idea of having me as a daughter-in-law, though a little concerned about my lack of duchess-like attributes. However, I'm not entirely sure that taking me to *The Ritz* to practice my airs and graces is going to be particularly helpful. Especially if she's wearing different coloured shoes.

The only thing that made me question my decision though was Sebastian's revelation about Ducal inheritance laws. Well, in all honesty, they weren't anything I didn't already know after digging into his family tree last year, but the thought that any son we have, would become the next Duke... Well, that's taken some getting used to. I'm already worrying about the possible stresses such a burden could place on a child that hasn't even been born yet.

But of course, we might not have a son at all. I think back to Tory's comment about twin girls in our family. Sebastian's assured me he's fully accepted the possibility that the title might finish with him, and secretly I can't help but hope we do have girls. After all, being an heir to a dynasty is not all it's cracked up to be. Just ask my brother.

At the beginning of December, my father comes to stay with my uncle and Mabel. It's not the first time he's been down since I moved to Dartmouth, but it's the first time he's met Sebastian.

Fortunately, my dad is nothing at all like the Admiral and the day Seb and I spent with him – just the three of us – was lovely. There were a few moments of disquiet – the first when he asked if I'd heard anything from my mother. By unspoken agreement, we told him nothing about *Operation Nick Nack* (as we've all ended up calling it) and, in fairness, he seemed relieved. I'd hate to think he'd been carrying a torch for her all these years. In all honesty, I hadn't realised quite how frail he was.

I think he liked Sebastian, and he especially enjoyed being invited to *Dinner with the Duke*. Nevertheless, he watched me carefully when he asked if I thought I was doing the right thing. My father is mild-mannered, especially when compared to the Admiral, but it doesn't mean he's stupid. In fairness, I think on balance, I'd have been better to have inherited his traits rather than the overbearing, cavalier, not giving a shit, characteristics of my one and only uncle.

Talking of which, said uncle has announced that he intends to hold an engagement party up at the Admiralty. Given the traits I've just listed, I don't know whether to be pleased or just plain terrified. Fortunately, Tory has promised to keep him in check – at least until the more blue-blooded of Sebastian's friends have drunk enough to ensure they won't remember. Much…

And I have a new frock. It's a simple black off the shoulder number that skims my curves in all the right places. This is the first sort of designer piece I've ever purchased in my life. In fairness, it *is* second-hand, and not quite *Prada*, but for someone whose wardrobe consisted of three men's suits just over a year ago, it's a massive leap forward.

And you know what? I really do look the business. I don't think I've ever appreciated that sometimes, being Junoesque can actually be a good thing. In fact, as I slip on my four-inch heels and look directly into the slumbering heat of Sebastian's eyes, I feel like I could take on the world. Naturally, the mood only lasts until I almost break my neck on the way to the car, but still …

The Admiralty was built for upmarket cocktail parties. In the flickering lamplight, the faded wallpaper and flaking paint disappear into the shadows, and with the huge Christmas tree in the drawing room, it feels as though we've been transported to a bygone era – à la Agatha Christie. I just hope nobody gets murdered before the end of the night. It would certainly put a damper on the proceedings, and the Admiral is hardly Hercule Poirot, despite his aspirations.

My other Dartmothians have scrubbed up surprisingly well too, and as we share a bottle of fizz before the nobility arrives, I'm overcome by the now familiar *warm and fuzzy*. The difference is, I no longer feel the need to fight it.

That said, it's probably fortunate that before I get too overcome with emotion, I overhear the strident tones of my uncle saying, 'Now remember Mabel, you'll be mixing with England's finest, and I know that when you usually open your mouth it's only to exchange what-ever foot's in there, so just talk about the weather and don't mention your bunion. Emily, try not to be too much of a Gatling gob, and if you happen to get hungry, go for the bunny grub – nobody really wants to eat carrot sticks in bloody December. Jimmy, I know you've got no ambition in life apart from breathing, but try to keep the conversation flowing and that means no talking about your bollocking nose miners.'

He pauses before adding, 'I think I've just about covered everything. Just remember, there's a definite knack to all this etiquette lark, but all you have to do is follow my lead. If there's one thing I know about, it's how to behave with royalty. Right then, Jimmy, go and fetch me a beer, will you, I'm as dry as a popcorn fart.'

* * *

I'M LYING IN BED, Coco one side of me and Sebastian on the other. Despite the lateness of the hour, I'm wide awake - mostly due to the ache in my shoulder. I know I've overdone it – truthfully, I should have had my arm in a sling. But pride goeth before a fall and all that ...

The evening was a huge success and for once it wasn't actually *despite* my actions. Tonight, I discovered a witty side of me that had Freddy muttering, 'who are you and what have you done with our techy Teddy?'

Nevertheless, despite all these new and exciting facets of my character, I lie here, wondering whether I might have bitten off more than I can chew. Sebastian's friends were nice enough. Polite in a *she doesn't look like a sumo wrestler* kind of way, but I'm not part of their world, and tonight simply emphasised that. They take so much for granted. Growing up with collective silver spoons, they are in a clique that no one like me will ever fit into. They start and finish each other's sentences, know all the same jokes about all the same people. How long will it be before I become another witty story for them to tell? Likely, the anecdotes about my mother are already doing the rounds.

And since I've not yet really been up to engagement ring hunting …

I know Seb doesn't care. After all's said and done, I could hardly be worse than his first wife and I do count an 'A' list, world famous actor as one of my friends. But nevertheless, however much Sebastian keeps himself apart – these people are his contemporaries. And there will be times when I have to get out of my comfort zone and be his duchess. If I love him like I claim to do, how can I do anything else? Tonight was simply a prelude of what's to come.

Sighing, I turn over gingerly and hug Coco to me with my good arm. She gives me a sleepy lick.

The question is, can I do it? The next big test will be our wedding day. And all joking aside, there may well be actual members of the Royal family present. How bloody ridiculous is that? I *really* don't know whether to laugh or cry…

Just before dawn, I fall into an uneasy doze and when I finally wake up at nearly nine a.m., and Sebastian is gone. Coco's still here though, which is a good indication that he isn't about to call off our engagement - and despite my soul searching, the relief that swamps me is unmistakable. As is the note he's left on his pillow.

Have some business to take care of sweetheart. Will be gone all day, so don't hold dinner for me. There's leftover chicken curry in the fridge. Love you xxx

Frowning, I manoeuvre myself into a sitting position. I know Alex isn't expecting me in the office today, but my mother-in-law to be, will be expecting a five-hundred-word article for next week's Herald, including intimate details of the party, and as much smutty stuff as I can invent without making us liable - or me a complete pariah before I've even joined the club. And since my refusal to do it will simply mean she does it herself, I think it would be better coming from me, even if I have to do it one-handed ...

I lay Seb's note back on his pillow and climb out of bed, much to Coco's displeasure. As I head to the bathroom, I can't help wondering exactly what business Sebastian is taking care of ...

CHAPTER 20

*I*t's the day before Christmas Eve and we're heading up to Bloodstone Tower in a private jet, no less. It's actually courtesy of our world-famous actor. Despite having a family lineage stretching back to the Conqueror, Seb informed me that the closest he could get to such luxury was Upper Class on EasyJet. When I told him I didn't think EasyJet did Upper Class, he grinned and said, 'Exactly.'

There will be thirteen of us travelling up altogether and I can't remember when I last looked forward to Christmas quite so much. Aside from the last couple of years, I've spent most of my adult life helping out in various homeless shelters on Christmas Day. When I was younger, I went along with my dad, but once I started working for the NCA, I went alone to the shelter nearest my flat in London. In fairness, neither Dad nor I had much time for the festive season after my mum left.

But now, well, now ... it's a new era. One that actually includes friends and family.

Despite my late-night agonising, I've said nothing to Sebastian about my fears. I've got plenty of time to get used to the idea of a big society wedding – at the end of the day, we haven't even booked it yet and the way Daphne was talking, it's going to take an army of staff to make sure the whole thing runs smoothly. I don't even know whether Seb wants it to be at Blackmore and in all honesty, I'm too nervous to ask him.

We'll talk about it in the New Year.

The flight is a lively affair with Christmas music playing throughout. We have canapés and cocktails and by the time we reach Glasgow, Freddy at least is a little merry. He changed from his jeans into kilt number one as soon as we were airborne, but he's already grumbling about the draft. I think Jason had earlier recommended he bring some long johns – but Freddy flatly refused, aghast that a true Scot could even suggest such a thing.

I think he might be rethinking his stance once we reach the High-lands, especially since according to the weather forecast, it's already started snowing.

Tory introduces us to Kit's Aunt Flo and her partner, Neil. Initially, I think she's nothing like I imagined the author of a bookcase full of bonkbusters would be – aside from the fact that her little dog Pepé has a proclivity for humping everything that moves - but after watching her making copious notes during a particularly risqué story Noah shares about his last movie, I revise my opinion. Naturally, he swears us all to secrecy – or at the very least, a change of names.

After landing in Glasgow airport, we still have another hour to travel – this time in a luxury coach with fully reclining seats and ear plugs. After the revelry on the plane, nearly everyone falls asleep within ten minutes of leaving the airport. Seb and I doze off with Coco snuggled between us. She's exhausted after catching up with Dotty and Pickles, not to mention putting Pepé in his place …

However, I'm fully awake again by the time we reach Loch Long and both Seb and I gaze spellbound at the lush dark forests and snow-shrouded peaks surrounding the loch.

I know that Sebastian has been looking for an excuse to come up to Scotland after discovering that Nicholas Sinclair, our missing Duke from last year, actually had an estate near Loch Lomond. According to the records we've since unearthed, he gave it over to his daughter, Jennifer and her husband, Brendon. With all the disruption caused by my mother, he hasn't had the time to pursue his research, but I know he'd love it if we could both explore Loch Lomond while we're here.

When we finally turn into the long narrow drive leading towards Bloodstone Tower, my excitement goes up a notch. I've heard so much about Jason's ancestral home and I really don't want to miss my first sighting.

'Remember when we first saw it Victory?' the Admiral comments. 'It looks a bloody sight better now than it did then.'

'I remember,' Freddy interrupted with a shudder. 'Three o'clock in the bloody morning, it was.'

'O'crack-sparrowfart,' Tory chuckles. I've no idea what she means, but I can't help noticing her gaze is a little sad as she looks over at Noah.

Seconds later, the road bends round and Bloodstone Tower suddenly appears directly in front of us. Its sheer size is breathtaking, and the backdrop of dark silent water and brooding mountains is enough to inspire the most gothic fairytale.

'Wow,' Sebastian breathes, delight evident in every movement. As the coach stops, the huge main door opens to reveal Jason and a man and woman I've never met before. There's a lot of hugging and patting of backs as we all pile out of the coach. 'Kit's taking a leaf out of her best friend's book and securing her place by the fire,' Jason grins, pulling Tory into a hug, before swinging a squealing Isaac into the air.

Then, tucking Isaac under his arm, he turns to me and Sebastian. 'This is my father, Hugo Buchannan,' he announces, 'and this lovely lady is our head housekeeper, Aileen.' I realise suddenly that we're the only two who haven't been here before.

Jason's father is a man around the Admiral's age with a shock of red hair. His welcoming hug is enthusiastic, and he doesn't confine it to me. Clearly, Hugo Buchannan doesn't believe in standing on ceremony.

'Och, it's guid tae meet ye.' Aileen's greeting is full of warmth, but not quite as tactile.

As we all pile through the huge front door, I can't help but stop and gape. The door leads directly into the Tower's great hall. With a high cavernous ceiling, flagstone floor, rich brocade curtains and tapestries, and finally a huge roaring fire, I feel as though we've stepped into the set of *Braveheart*. I've never seen anything like it – not even Blackmore is this awe-inspiring. The Christmas decorations look as though they've sprung from the pages of *House Beautiful*, with garland after garland of evergreen foliage contrasting with deep red baubles, lengths of velvet ribbon and zillions of fairy lights. The huge fir tree in the corner nearly touches the ceiling, and almost every inch is decorated the same way. Both the smell and the overall effect are simply amazing.

I turn to Seb who's gazing round with his mouth open, just like me. I can't help but smile - it's not often I see him completely forget his manners.

'I'd be delighted to show you around later,' Jason offers with a knowing grin. 'The Hall can be a little overwhelming when you first walk in.'

'Truly, it's magnificent, Jason,' Seb enthuses. 'I'd love to see everything.'

'You can thank my wife for her vision and my silent partner for his money,' Jason retorts, laughing. 'I just got my hands dirty.'

'I got my hands dirty on more than one occasion,' Noah argues, taking a wriggling Isaac out of his friend's arms while keeping a close eye on the twins. They've just started walking and have a tendency to get into everything.

'In the summer,' Jason scoffs. 'That doesn't count.'

I walk towards the cavernous fireplace where Tory has already commandeered baby Hugo, hovered over by Flo who is anxiously waiting her turn. I smile and lean down to give Kit a hug. She looks tired, but happy, and ever truthful, I tell her exactly that, though the new improved me uses the word *radiant*, rather than happy. She laughs, clearly seeing through my attempt at a positive spin, but nevertheless gives my hand a grateful squeeze.

The sofas and armchairs are strategically placed for everyone to get reasonably close to the fire, and we jostle for position as Aileen brings in a tray of tea, closely followed by a young girl bearing a huge plate of shortbread.

'What, no tablet, Aileen?' Tory demands in mock horror.

'Ah'll nae be responsible fer ye losin' yer teeth wi' that evil stuff,' Aileen sniffs. 'At least it'll take a while longer wi the shortbread.'

I've no idea what *tablet* is, but assume it contains a large amount of sugar. As Seb and I sit down, Tory turns towards us. 'You have to try some of Aileen's shortbread,' she enthuses. 'It's truly to die for.' Obligingly, we help ourselves to a large piece each. She's right. A year ago I'd have said it was better than sex …

'While I fully intend to take my hostess duties seriously,' Kit announces gravely, 'all directing will take place from here. And, unless they wish to spend the remainder of the holiday in the dungeon below us, no one but me is to put their posterior on my seat …' She pauses and shifts with a small wince before adding, 'Or my whoopy cushion …'

For a second, we're all silent, contemplating the chain of events that have culminated in an actual whoopy cushion, then Kit gives a wide grin and says, 'It's bloody marvellous to have you all here. We're going to have a wonderful Christmas.'

An hour later, we're shown up to our rooms with orders to rest before dinner. Drinks are being served at seven.

Our bedroom is beautiful. The fourposter bed, though clearly authentic, has an up to the minute sprung mattress. Just as Coco gathers herself to try it out, I shake my head and point to her basket. 'No dogs on the hotel bed, sweetie.' I soften my order by getting onto my hands and knees to kiss the end of her nose as she grumpily curls up in her bed.

Like the great hall, the furniture is art nouveau, but here the walls are papered with Rennie Mackintosh roses, echoed in the lamps and statement pieces dotted around the room. In contrast, the bathroom is ultra-modern with clean lines and a shower that could accommodate half a dozen people.

'It's like a honeymoon suite,' I exclaim, then could have bitten out my tongue.

'Maybe we could come up to Bloodstone Tower for our honeymoon,' Sebastian suggests, pushing the door shut with his back before putting down our heavy cases with obvious relief. 'How long did you say we're planning on stopping?' He clearly doesn't feel any discomfort talking about our wedding, and I silently berate myself. When the bloody hell did I become such a sensitive Sally? He walks over and gathers me into his arms, and I can't help but notice he's breathing a little heavily and I look at him enquiringly.

'Spiral stairs aren't for the faint-hearted,' he clarifies.

I lean away from him and raise my eyebrows. 'Or the elderly, obviously.'

He grins down at me. 'I think Jason's having a bespoke lift built up the side of the Tower, but until that happens, there'll be no throwing you down on the bed and ravishing you.'

'Spoilsport,' I grin back. 'So, no little nap then?'

'I didn't say that,' he murmurs, allowing his lips to brush mine.

'I don't mind waiting until you get your breath back,' I whisper.

His eyes narrow, but instead of answering, he bends his head again. His kiss is still light, tantalising, but this time he eases his hand between us and cups my breast through my shirt, rubbing his thumb lazily back and forth across my nipple. I groan and press myself against him. 'Perhaps I *should* spend a little time getting my breath back,' he breathes, now pressing soft, featherlight kisses along my jaw and down to my neck. My breath hitches and I shake my head, circling my hips against his arousal in protest.

He gives a soft laugh and moves me backwards until the back of my legs hit the bed. Then he gives a slight push and we both tumble onto the soft coverlet, his hand carefully supporting my shoulder. This time his mouth meets mine in a kiss that hardly leaves any room for breathing, while his free hand slips underneath my shirt to cup my bare skin. I inhale sharply and instinctively lift my breasts to his questing fingers, my low moan becoming almost a cry as he rolls my erect nipple in between his thumb and forefinger. Sensation slams through me and I drag my mouth away to scoot up the bed, ignoring the pain in my arm to pull at my jeans as I go. When my legs are free, he yanks hard at my panties, baring me to his heated gaze. Slowly, his eyes never leaving mine, he frees himself from his own jeans and nudging open my legs, he first kneels above me, then lowers himself until I can feel his hardness between my legs. I give a small whimper and lift my hips. 'Please,' I whisper.

He gives another soft laugh and gradually eases himself forward until he's buried deep inside me. I close my eyes, revelling in the welcoming fullness, wondering how it can get any better than this. Until, slowly, deliberately, he begins to move, showing me exactly how …

CHAPTER 21

*D*inner is a chaotic and lively affair with anecdotes coming thick and fast from all around the table. Now that Bloodstone Tower has a full-time chef and a team of kitchen staff, both Aileen and the new hotel manager, Kevan, are able to join us at the table. Though quite whether they'll want to do it again remains to be seen...

The children are contributing to the chaos, with more food ending up on the floor than in little mouths, much to Dotty, Pickles, Coco and Pepé's collective delight. And throughout it all Hugo sleeps the blissful sleep of all newborns. Kit predicts he'll be awake as soon as they get into bed.

As I look over at Sebastian, I wish with all my heart that we could simply get married here, with all our friends and close family, but nobody else. But I know it's impossible and, more than that, it would be hugely unfair to ask him. By accepting his proposal, I've agreed to embrace customs and traditions that have been in place for centuries. I want to marry Sebastian – I really do. But I'm just not sure I can deal with the pomp and ceremony of a society wedding.

I clench my hands together, forcing my mind away from the thought of the hundreds of people Daphers will insist on inviting.

'Are you okay, sweetheart?' Seb asks, as ever attuned to my shifting moods. I smile back at him.

'My shoulder's aching a little, that's all.' It's not a lie. Our horizontal exercise earlier definitely left it throbbing. But two ibuprofen and a nice hot shower have since reduced it to a slight twinge.

'You've been through quite the ordeal over the last few weeks,' Flo comments. 'Charlie has been telling me all about it.' I look over at the Admiral who's looking decidedly sheepish.

'And, of course, my uncle hasn't embellished it even the teensiest bit,' I respond drily ...

'Stuff of fiction,' she agrees with a sympathetic smile, 'but don't worry, I won't write about it.'

'You'll have to join the queue,' I quip.

'If you need an agent, give me a shout,' Neil grins. 'We might be able to sell it to *Netflix*.'

'Or put it on the stage,' Freddy pipes up. '*Teddy Shackleford – the Musical…*'

Fortunately for me, the conversation grinds to a halt as Ember chooses that moment to tip her bowl of custard over her head. 'I think we'd better get these three in the bath,' Tory gasps, whisking the bowl away before the trickle down her daughter's neck becomes a tsunami. 'If we take their clothes off in the bath,' she suggests to Noah, 'we'll be able to get the excess debris off before we put them in the wash.'

'Don't you dare.' Freddy's voice is aghast as he points his finger at Tory accusingly. 'What colour are the twins' dresses likely to come out if you commit such a hideous crime? I'll have you know I got those outfits from *Ralph Lauren*.'

Tory frowns, looking between her three offspring, seemingly baffled by the question.

'The dresses are *pale blue* and Isaac's trousers are *dark red*,' Freddy almost yells. 'I cannot, and will not allow you to commit such a crime.' Pushing back his chair, he climbs to his feet while rolling up his sleeves. 'Bring them to me one at a time,' he orders, before stomping off towards the stairs.

Seconds later, the door slams behind him.

Kit raises her eyebrows. 'I think you've upset him,' she grins.

Tory winces. 'I'd better go and apologise,' she sighs. 'I admit, I turned a blind eye after Tobi put cauliflower cheese in Isaac's hair. I'll take the cleanest one up first.' She pauses for a second before adding, 'Which one looks the cleanest to you?' Not knowing who she's asking, we collectively study all three children – who are, in fact, liberally covered in a variety of foodstuffs. 'I was doing so well up until then,' Tory adds wistfully.

'I think that was about the time you had your third glass of wine,' Alex chuckles.

'I'd drop 'em in the bloody loch,' the Admiral states, eying all three grandchildren with distaste.

'If my parenting skills leave a bit to be desired, you can see why,' Tory retorts huffily.

'There's nothing wrong with your parenting skills, or mine, honey,' Noah protests, while obviously trying not to laugh. 'It's the kids' holiday too'

'And the dogs,' Sebastian grins. 'Their Christmas has definitely started early.'

'Why not strip them down to their nappies, *then* take them upstairs to Freddy,' I suggest. 'I'll help if you like?'

Nobody is more surprised by my offer than me. Well, in fairness, that's not quite true if the incredulous looks I'm receiving are anything to go by.

Tory gives me a broad smile. 'That's okay, Teddy. Enjoy the freedom while it lasts. Remember, it's double the fun for all of us with Shackleford genes.'

'That's an old wife's tale' I scoff – not for the first time.

'You keep telling yourself that,' she answers with a wink – also not for the first time.

'Quickest way to build a netball team,' Alex laughs.

'What about basketball?' Jason suggests. 'Especially if they're over six feet.'

'Oh, I don't think even Teddy's likely to give birth to a baby that big,' Mabel protests earnestly.

There's a small silence, then Tory gives an almost strangled cough and jumps to her feet. Minutes later, the three children are naked apart from their nappies.

'He said to bring them one at a time,' Alex reminds her and Noah.

'I'm not sure how many children Freddy has actually bathed up to now,' is Tory's scathing retort, 'but trust me, unless he wants to be there all night, he'll put them in together - while we wait to fish then out.' She picks up the discarded clothes off the floor. 'I'll leave these outside his door.'

After dinner, Sebastian suggests we take the dogs out for a quick walk before having an early night. I'm surprised – not by the dog walk, but by his suggestion of an early night until I realise that he's thinking about my recovery. Warmed by his concern, I smile and get to my feet.

'Don't worry about Pepe. If we mention *walkies* to him, it'll take us the rest of the night to find out where he's hiding.' Flo gently strokes the small dog, currently comatose on her lap.

Since my uncle and Mabel are propped up against each other, fast asleep, I assume it's okay to take Pickles along. Dotty, too, seems more than happy to have a quick jaunt outside.

'I wouldn't go far,' Jason warns. 'It's bitter out there, and the mist can come down very suddenly. I don't want to be fishing your frozen corpse out of the loch.'

'It would definitely put a damper on the Christmas cheer,' Seb observes drily. 'You want to join us, Alex?'

He shudders and shakes his head. 'Hot-house flower. I blame my Caribbean roots.'

'Mmm, sounds like an interesting storyline,' Flo is musing as we put on our coats. *The Body in the Loch...*' Her voice fades away as we step outside into the darkness. Jason's right – it is bloody freezing.

'Right then, brisk walk down to the water's edge and back,' Sebastian suggests. I nod, pulling on my gloves as I follow him down the narrow path. But despite our determination to make it quick, when we reach the Loch side, we're transfixed. The sky is literally full of stars – enough to make you dizzy if you look too long. Sebastian informs me that the moon is waxing, but it's full enough to light up the loch and cause the snow along its banks to sparkle and shine.

'It looks like Narnia,' I breathe, looking around in awe. Sebastian nods but doesn't answer. Instead, he puts his arm around my shoulders and tucks me in to him. He's always been good at silence. After about ten minutes, though, I can't suppress a shiver, and Seb feels it. While Pickles and Coco are still sniffing around, Dotty is standing on the path, her opinion of the whole experience very clear.

'Alright, Dotspot,' he laughs, 'We get that you've had enough.' Then he leans over to give me a cold, damp kiss before pulling me back up the path. 'Time for bed.'

For some reason I wake up before it's fully light the next morning. For several moments, I lay disoriented in the pre-dawn darkness, my eyes travelling over unfamiliar shapes as I try to work out where I am. As awareness returns, I turn my head to the side and realise that Sebastian is missing.

Frowning, fully awake now, I sit up. Coco isn't in her basket either. Likely he's gone to take her out for a wee. I lay back down again. Strange that she's awake this early, though. But then, I suppose it's not that early for her. Daybreak in Scotland during the winter comes a lot later than in South Devon and she's in a strange place, bless her. It's not surprising she's a bit restless. I wonder if I should get out of bed and look for them. Then I stick my right leg out from under the covers and shiver. Nope - whatever it is they're up to, as long as I get a cup of tea when they return, I'm content. Snuggling back down, I pull the covers up over my shoulders, turn over, and go back to sleep.

When I next wake, it's fully light outside, but Sebastian and Coco are still missing. Blinking, I feel the first sense of disquiet and lean over to look at my phone. It's just after nine thirty. Perhaps Seb thought I'd enjoy a lie in. But he knows me better than that. I *hate* missing anything. Frowning, I climb out of bed. The room is warm now but rather than go to the window naked I slip on Seb's shirt before hurrying to look outside ...

... Where there's a line of delivery vans and several strangers milling about. I stare for a few minutes, wondering what the hell is going on, then I suddenly cotton on. Clearly, Kit and Jason are taking the deliveries for tomorrow and no doubt Sebastian is helping them. Chuckling at my ridiculous feeling of unease, I turn back to the bed. If I go and shower now, I might be in time to lend a hand.

I'm just about to shrug off the shirt when there's a sudden knock at the door. Seconds later, it opens to admit Kit and Tory. I stare at them in confusion, shirt half off my shoulders.

Without being asked, they walk into the room with a pile of clothing which they lay reverently on the bed. Behind them, Freddy trots in with a hairdryer and a set of straighteners. Finally, Aileen enters carrying a large tray with a bottle of Champagne sitting in an ice bucket, a bottle of fresh orange juice and three glasses. Oh, and a large plate of shortbread. Then, with a wink, she backs out, closing the door behind her.

The only one in the room not smiling is me.

Kit goes to the tray and pours out four glasses of bucks fizz. She hands one to Freddy, one to Tory, and one to me. Mechanically, I take it and she finally picks up one for herself.

All three of them raise their glasses. 'Welcome to your wedding day, Teddy,' Tory says with a giddy laugh. I stare at them bewildered, then I sit down on the bed. Hard.

Did I mention I hate surprises?

* * *

THE REST of the day feels almost like a dream. I'd wished so hard for a small, intimate wedding with only the people I love around me. And, like always, Sebastian knew it. He *knew* I didn't want the big society wedding, and my wishes were more important to him than age-old customs and traditions.

I have a choice of three dresses and choose the one from the top – they know me well, these friends of mine. Off the shoulder, with long sleeves, fitted to the waist and flaring over my hips in an A-line skirt. The underskirt is the palest grey, with white lace over the bodice.

My bouquet is white gypsophila and Christmas roses.

Freddy does the best he can with my hair and make-up – at the end of the day, he can only work with what he's been given. But when I look at myself in the mirror, for the first time in the whole of my life, I feel completely beautiful.

As Freddy puts the last finishing touches to my hair, there's another knock at the door. Tory swiftly opens it to reveal the Dowager Duchess.

Did I mention I don't like surprises?

Daphers walks up, takes my face in her hands and whispers, 'Make him happy.' Then she hands a diamond comb to Freddy. I gaze at it wordlessly, wondering how many former duchesses have worn it. Did Grace Shackleford wear it when she married Nicholas? Or perhaps Jennifer, her daughter. I swallow and manage to thank my soon to be mother-in-law through my tears as Freddy threads the comb into my hair. Seconds later, the door closes behind her.

There's just the four of us, along with the warm and fuzzy I've come to expect. Freddy keeps me laughing, while Kit and Tory put on their bridesmaid's dresses. 'It's not like you have a lot of choice, I'm afraid,' Kit tells me as she struggles into her dress. 'Bugger, I'm never going to get pregnant again.'

Tory, on the other hand, amazingly, slips easily into hers. 'OMG, this is a first,' she crows. 'Freddy, take a photo.' We have another drink and a few minutes later, there's yet another knock on the door. It's Freddy's turn to answer it, and in walks my father.

Did I mention I don't like surprises?

This time I do cry, and both Kit and Tory ply me with tissues, since walking down the aisle with mascara on my cheeks is most definitely not a good look.

'You look beautiful, Theodora,' he whispers, holding out his arm. I give a sniff, then slip my arm into his as Tory hands me my bouquet.

We descend the staircase carefully, and when Tory finally pushes open the door to the great hall, I start crying for real. Everyone I love is here. And *only* everyone I love. As I walk toward Sebastian, I hardly even notice the registrar. All my carefully prepared make up is sliding down my face. I catch sight of Freddy's panicked face and suddenly laugh. Stopping, I wait for him to mop me up, then I continue down the aisle to the love of my life.

Twenty minutes later, I'm the new Duchess of Blackmore.

Seb tells me later that he was terrified I'd cry off if I was forced to do the society wedding.

He's wrong, I wouldn't have. But I don't tell him that. I'm content to simply bask in the fairytale.

And when the ceremony is over, I turn and embrace the extraordinary people who trampled all over my former life and remade it into something wonderful.

Maybe surprises aren't so bad after all.

EPILOGUE

'*J*'m not entirely certain it's quite the thing for the Duchess of Blackmore to be working for a newspaper.'

I frown at my mother-in-law. 'I don't think Sebastian has a problem with it, and honestly, Daphers, I'll go bonkers if I have to play Lady of the Manor without any distractions.' She purses her lips and sighs as I deliver the punchline. 'And anyway, why is it okay for you to dig out the dirt, but not me?'

'Darling, I'm the eccentric mother. One day I'm certain you'll be that too. But until then, we have to protect your reputation.'

I grit my teeth, preparing to argue further when there's a sudden knock on the office door.

Alex, who's prudently kept quiet until now, goes to open it. To my complete surprise, standing on the other side is the Admiral.

'I need your help, Teddy,' he blurts, hurrying inside.

'What on earth's the matter, Uncle Charlie?' I climb to my feet, wondering if someone's died. 'Sit down. Would you like some tea?'

189

'No, I don't want any bollocking tea.' He's almost sobbing and my anxiety ratches up a notch. What on earth could have happened?

'Tell me concisely and clearly exactly what's wrong,' I order him calmly.

'You know that DNA testing kit Mabel bought me for Christmas?' He sounds as though he's on the verge of a breakdown and I rest my hand on his reassuringly.

'Of course,' I murmur soothingly, looking over at Alex with raised eyebrows.

'Well, I did it and sent it away. So did Jimmy.' He briefly puts his head into his hands, a picture of despair, before looking back up and grabbing hold of my arm. 'Teddy, I don't know what to do. It turns out we're bloody related.'

I open my mouth and close it again. What the bloody hell am I supposed to say?

'Is that a problem?' I manage at length.

'Well, of course it's a bollocking problem. It's a complete bloody cake and arse party. I need you to look into it for me, Teddy. I need you to prove them wrong.'

'I'm not quite sure I can help you, Uncle,' I begin. 'The thing is …'

'… I'm certain we can come to some agreement about your future employment,' Daphne cuts in smoothly. 'Admiral Shackleford, would you like a glass of Champagne?'

THE END

AUTHOR'S NOTES

While I have, as always, taken liberties, the problems facing the Japanese Imperial family are real – as are the possible remedies the Japanese Government are currently considering. If you're interested in the more recent history of the crisis, head to Google – there are many, many articles detailing the issues faced.

As I've said in my previous books, if you ever find yourself in the Southwest of England, the beautiful yachting haven of Dartmouth in South Devon is well worth a visit. The pubs and restaurants I describe are real, and I've spent many a happy lunchtime/evening in each of them. If you'd like more information about Dartmouth and the surrounding areas, you can go to the following website for the Tourist Information Centre:
https://discoverdartmouth.com

And the second location in Final Victory...
Loch Long in the glorious Scottish Highlands does exist – although I've yet to come across Bloodstone Tower! The loch itself is a beautiful sea loch surrounded by mountains. It forms the entire western

coastline of the Rosneath Peninsula in Western Scotland, an area so
magnificent it will take your breath away...
For more information about Loch Long and the Rosneath Peninsula,
click on the link below:
http://www.trossachs.co.uk/loch-long.php

KEEPING IN TOUCH

Thank you so much for reading Final Victory, I really hope you
enjoyed it.
For any of you who'd like to connect, I'd really love to hear from you.
Feel free to contact me via my facebook page:
https://www.facebook.com/beverleywattsromanticcomedyauthor
or my website:
http://www.beverleywatts.com

If you'd like me to let you know as soon as my next book is available,
copy and paste the link below into your browser to sign up to my
newsletter and I'll keep you updated about that and all my latest
releases.

https://motivated-teacher-3299.ck.page/143a008c18

For those of you who haven't yet given the Shackleford Sisters a go
but would like to know how the Duke of Blackmore came to marry a
vicar's daughter, Grace: Book One of The Shackleford Sisters is
available from Amazon.

Turn the page for a sneak peek...

GRACE

....Reverend Augustus Shackleford's mission in life (aside from ensuring the collection box was suitably full every Sunday) was to secure advantageous marriages for each of his eight daughters. A tall order, given the fact that in the Reverend's opinion they didn't possess a single ladylike bone in the eight bodies they had between them. Quite where he would find a wealthy titled gentleman bottle headed enough to take any of them on remained a mystery and indeed was likely to test even his legendary resourcefulness.

....Grievously wounded at the Battle of Trafalgar, Nicholas Sinclair was only recently returned to Blackmore after receiving news of his estranged father's unexpected death. After an absence of twenty years, the new Duke was well aware it was his duty to marry and produce an heir as quickly as possible. However, tormented by recurring nightmares after his horrific experiences during the battle, Nicholas had no taste to brave the ton's marriage mart in search of a docile obedient wife.

.....Never in his wildest dreams did Reverend Shackleford envisage receiving an offer for his eldest daughter from the new Duke of Blackmore. Of course, the Reverend was well aware he was fudging it a bit in describing Grace as respectful, meek or dutiful, nevertheless, he could never have imagined that his eldest daughter's unruliness might end up ruining them all....

Prologue

The Reverend Augustus Shackleford rested his hands contentedly on his ample stomach and belched loudly, the stew he'd just consumed resting a trifle heavily on his stomach. It was noon at the Red Lion Pub in the village of Blackmore in Devonshire, England, and while he could have quite easily have had his luncheon back at the vicarage, the Reverend much preferred the ale and conversation the pub provided as opposed to the never-ending arguing and bickering that came with the unfortunate position of having nine females residing in his house. Though he'd never asked him, the Reverend was content that his dog Freddy was also of the same opinion. The foxhound was currently curled up under the table, happily chasing rabbits in his dreams.

Reverend Shackleford was not a man of immense wealth and fortune, and under normal circumstances would be quite content with the fact that the coin in his pocket would more than suffice the cost of the meal he had just consumed.

These were not normal circumstances, however, and the coin in his pocket – or anywhere else for that matter, would certainly not be sufficient to provide the money to set up his only son in the manner befitting a gentleman.

His only son after eight daughters. The Reverend sighed. It had taken three wives to finally produce an heir, but the cost of paying for the eight females he'd been blessed with in the first instance was sorely testing even his creativity – something he'd prided himself on up until now.

He sat morosely staring into his pint of ale next to his long-suffering curate and only friend, Percy Noon.

"You know me Percy, I've got a mind as sharp as a well-creased cravat, but I've got to admit I'm completely nonplussed as to what to do to raise the coin."

"Perhaps you can find some kind of work for your daughters, something suitable in polite society for ladies of a gentle disposition," Percy suggested as he pushed his tin plate aside.

The Reverend snorted. "Have you seen any of my daughters lately?" he scoffed, shaking his head glumly. "Ladies of a gentle disposition? They don't possess a single ladylike bone in the eight bodies they have between 'em. They have no clue how to follow orders or how to comport themselves in any society, let alone a polite one.

"If I wish to secure even a modest fortune for Anthony, then I have no recourse but to marry 'em off. Though I can't imagine a man who'd be foolish enough to encumber himself with any of 'em. Unless he was in his cups, of course." The Reverend was silent for a while, clearly imagining a scenario where he could take advantage of a well-heeled male whilst the unfortunate victim was suitably foxed. In the end, he sighed.

"Percy, the situation is dire indeed. If I don't come up with a plan soon, there's going to be no coin left for Anthony at all. And not only that, we could well find ourselves in the workhouse." He glared at Percy as if it was somehow all his curate's fault. "If that happens, Percy my man, there'll be no more bread-and-butter pudding for you of an evening. Percy repressed a shudder. He wasn't sure if it was at the prospect of ending up in the workhouse or the thought of Mrs. Tomlinson's bread and butter pudding – the last of which could probably have been used to shut out the drafts. The curate suspected the vicarage cook was a little too fond of Blue Ruin to give much attention to her culinary skills.

"Then your only recourse, Sir, is to marry them off and marry them well," he stated decisively, settling deeper into his chair. "Somehow."

The Reverend stroked his chin, thinking about his wayward daughters. Each daughter was entirely different than the last. The only similarity they all shared was unruliness. Four of them were already at a marriageable age, with the eldest, at twenty-five, a confirmed bluestocking. What chance did he have of marrying any of them off to a wealthy gentleman bacon-brained enough to secure a fortune for his only son?

He was sure that given time, he could do it. But it would test even his legendary resourcefulness. Especially if he was going to do it without spending any coin.

"Right, we'll need a list of suitable wealthy titled gentlemen bottle-headed enough to take 'em on Percy," he decided, motioning for another mug of ale. "Then we'll let 'em know that I have, err ... good, dutiful daughters who are in need of husbands."

"As you wish, Sir," Percy said doubtfully as the serving wench brought another ale for them both. The Reverend picked up his tankard and took a large gulp.

"But before we do that, we'll start by writing down all the positive attributes of the chits so that we can emphasize their good points to any prospective husbands. I mean we both know that none of them are exactly bachelor fare, but we can fudge it a bit without anyone being the wiser. At least until they have a ring on their finger.

"We'll start with Grace since she's the one most likely to end up an old maid if we don't come up with the goods pretty sharpish. Right then, Percy, you start."

Silence.

The Reverend frowned. "Come on man, surely you can find some-thing good to say about her."

'She has nicely turned ankles," responded Percy a bit desperately.

"Steady on Percy. I certainly hope you've never had an extended opportunity to observe my eldest daughter's ankles. Otherwise, I might have to call you out."

Percy reddened, flustered. "Oh no, Sir, not at all, I just happened to notice when she was climbing into the carria..."

"Humph, well I'm not sure we can put that at the top of the list, but in Grace's case, we might have to resort to it. I mean why her mother chose to call her Grace is beyond me, considering she's distinctly lacking in any attributes remotely divine-like. And she's the least graceful person I've ever come across. If there's something to trip over, Grace will find it. Clumsy doesn't even begin to cut it," he added gloomily.

"Well, she has very nice eyes," Percy stated, thinking it best to keep any further observations about the Reverend's daughter above the neck. "And her teeth are sound."

The Reverend nodded, scribbling furiously.

"Can she cook, Sir?" The Reverend stopped writing and frowned. "I don't know that she can, Percy. At least not in the same capacity as Mrs. Tomlinson."

"Probably best not to mention it then," Percy interrupted hastily, unwillingly conjuring up the vision of Mrs. Tomlinson's bread and butter pudding again. "And anyway, marriage to a gentleman is not likely to necessitate her venturing into the kitchen." The Reverend nodded thoughtfully.

"How about her voice? Can she sing?"

"Like a strangled cat."

"Dance?"

"I don't think she's ever danced with anyone. I deuced hope not anyway. If she has, I'll have his guts for garters."

"Conversation?" Percy was getting desperate.

"Nonexistent. I don't think she's spoken more than half a dozen words to me since she was in the crib." The Reverend was becoming increasingly despondent.

"Does she cut a good mother figure to her sisters?"

The Reverend snorted. "I don't think any of 'em are without some kind of scar where she's dropped 'em at some time or another."

"How about her brain?" Percy now resorted to clutching at straws.

"Now that's something the chit has got. Every time I see her, she's got her nose in a book. Problem is, that's the one attribute any well-heeled gentleman will most definitely not be looking for…"

Grace: Book One of The Shackleford Sisters is available from Amazon

ALSO BY BEVERLEY WATTS ON AMAZON

The Shackleford Diaries:
Book 1 - Claiming Victory
Book 2 - Sweet Victory
Book 3 - All for Victory
Book 4 - Chasing Victory
Book 5 - Lasting Victory
Book 6 - A Shackleford Victory
Book 7 - Final Victory

The Shackleford Sisters
Book 1- Grace
Book 2 - Temperance
Book 3 - Faith
Book 4 - Hope
Book 5 -Patience
Book 6 - Charity
Book 7 - Chastity
Book 8 - Prudence
Book 9 - Anthony

The Shackleford Legacies
Book 1 - Jennifer
Book 2 - Mercedes
Book 3 - Roseanna
Book 4 - Henrietta will be released on 20th December 2025

Shackleford and Daughters
Book 1 - Alexandra will be released on 12th June 2025

The Admiral Shackleford Mysteries
Book 1 - A Murderous Valentine
Book 2 - A Murderous Marriage
Book 3 - A Murderous Season

Standalone Titles
An Officer and a Gentleman Wanted

ABOUT THE AUTHOR

Beverley spent 8 years teaching English as a Foreign Language to International Military Students in Britannia Royal Naval College, the Royal Navy's premier officer training establishment in the UK. She says that in the whole 8 years there was never a dull moment and many of her wonderful experiences at the College were not only memorable but were most definitely 'the stuff of fiction.' Her debut novel An Officer And A Gentleman Wanted is very loosely based on her adventures at the College.

Beverley particularly enjoys writing books that make people laugh and currently she has three series of Romantic Comedies, both contemporary and historical, as well as a humorous cosy mystery series under her belt.

She lives with her husband in an apartment overlooking the sea on the beautiful English Riviera. Between them they have 3 adult children and two gorgeous grandchildren plus 3 Romanian rescue dogs of indeterminate breed called Florence, Trixie, and Lizzie. Until recently, they also had an adorable 'Chichon" named Dotty who was the inspiration for Dotty in The Shackleford Diaries.

You can find out more about Beverley's books at www.beverley-watts.com

Made in the USA
Monee, IL
09 April 2025

15459627R00115